Penguin Books
Hot Pursuit

Gavin Scott was born in England in 1950, but his
family emigrated to New Zealand when he was
eleven. He received most of his education at
Wanganui Collegiate School and Victoria University,
Wellington. He subsequently spent a year teaching
in Borneo with the Volunteer Service Abroad, and
was transport correspondent with NZBC. He also
produced a radio documentary series, *Insight*. In
1973 Gavin Scott came to London and worked for
two years on *The Times Educational Supplement*
before joining the BBC, where he is now a reporter
for *The World at One*.

Hot Pursuit is Mr Scott's first novel.

Gavin Scott

Hot Pursuit

Penguin Books

Penguin Books Ltd, Harmondsworth,
Middlesex, England
Penguin Books, 625 Madison Avenue,
New York, New York 10022, U.S.A.
Penguin Books Australia Ltd, Ringwood,
Victoria, Australia
Penguin Books Canada Ltd, 2801 John Street,
Markham, Ontario, Canada L3R 1B4
Penguin Books (N.Z.) Ltd, 182–190 Wairau Road,
Auckland 10, New Zealand

First published by
William Collins Sons & Company Ltd in their Crime Club 1977
Published in Penguin Books 1979

Made and printed in Great Britain by
Cox & Wyman Ltd,
London, Reading and Fakenham
Set in Intertype Times

To Jane
who began it

Contents

In recent years, when the leaders of one state wished to justify an armed incursion into a neighbouring state in pursuit of malefactors, they have made use of the phrase 'in hot pursuit'. They claim that a convention exists whereby, if the forces of one nation are 'in hot pursuit' of guerrillas and such like, they are entitled to enter the territory of a neighbour in order to apprehend them. The validity of the claim in international law is doubtful.

1 The Cone

There were three of us up on the rooftop, fifteen storeys above the city, and it would take a computer several valuable seconds to work out the odds against it. Each of us, for an instant, was motionless: me, against the fire-door; Hammersham, half-way across the expanse of white gravel, and the man in the boiler suit, ten feet from the edge, hunched over a white plastic cone, the wind filling his boiler suit as though someone was inflating it. It was a February day, the sky was black, and the wind came at us every thirty seconds or so, slapping like a big wet tarpaulin.

In those few seconds the nuclear pile went critical. Just as a certain combination of atomic units can turn a nuclear power station into a bomb, so the combination of those three figures, under a winter sky high above London, tipped the balance of our reaction away from control. And when that happened, all hell broke loose.

None of us should have been up there. I shouldn't have been up there because I'm not on the staff of Amalgamated National Newspapers, and I'm not even sure the staff are allowed on the roof anyway. I'd gone up to the fourth floor to see the news editor and I'd seen him and handed in my copy and signed an expenses claim, and as far as Amalgamated National Newspapers was concerned that was that until they wanted me again.

Actually, they would probably want me again fairly soon, because I worked for them regularly, and some of them even regarded me as one of the staff, but I wasn't. I was freelance, and not because I made more money that way. I freelanced for Hammersham's papers to keep afloat a small community news service I operate from a basement in North Kensington in a street they've been planning to knock down for a long time, and haven't got around to.

The stories my news service gathers are about things like that, and the editors of the sort of papers that print those stories never have any money to pay for them, and the result is I spend around forty per cent of my time working for Amalgamated National and all it stands for and the rest of the time working against it. To be fair, I like working for them; I like the people, I like the atmosphere. I just don't like the editorials.

So usually, when I've completed my stint, I relieve my feelings by stepping into the lift, riding up to the fifteenth floor, opening the fire-door, and stepping out on to the gravel to look at the view. And on this occasion I had company.

The view from the top of Amalgamated House is always dramatic, and on that dark February day it was even more impressive than usual. To the south St Paul's floated grey against the darkness of the sky like a huge balloon, ready at any moment to tear its anchor ropes and drift unsteadily off across the city on some long-pondered errand. To the east the Wren spires gleamed unnaturally, bone-white against the dull office-buildings around them. The Barbican tower blocks loomed to the north, storey after storey of balconies silhouetted like the teeth of a saw. Cloud covered most of the distant skyline of Parliament Hill, and from there a tide of slate-grey roofs and chimney pots flowed down to Holborn, bobbing with red domes and copper-green towers, swirling through Clerkenwell and over Saffron Hill along the streets where Oliver met Fagin, past Booth's Gin factory.

Hammersham wasn't looking at the view at all. His entire attention was concentrated on the man in the boiler suit, and from thirty feet away I could see that he was tense with fury.

Hammersham is a Lord and he owns Amalgamated Newspapers. He is a big man, born fifty years ago, with a face like an American eagle, heavy with good living, but not fat. His hair is black and thinning and his eyes are grey and hard. He inherited his newspaper empire, but keeping it has been a long fierce battle and he has fought that battle with ferocity and gusto. It sounds as though I knew him, but of course I didn't. I had contributed to quite a number of papers in his empire, and doubtless he had never read any of those contributions and certainly he had never heard of me. The only thing that brought us together was the random chance that he had decided to leave his fifteenth-floor office and smoke a cigar on the roof about sixty seconds before I stepped out through that fire-door.

What had brought him up short was the man in the boiler suit, because the man in the boiler suit was very obviously bugging the building. He might have been a workman but he wasn't. The white plastic cone in his hand might have been the cover of one of the dozens of ventilator shafts which sprouted through the gravel like orderly mushrooms. But it wasn't. Ventilator covers do not contain mechanisms requiring delicate attention with a screwdriver, and to fit them you do not need to have an earphone in your ear. Hammersham saw this and it made him angry. Because the bug was being installed directly above his own office.

It was only an instant during which we were all motionless, but it seemed longer. I was frozen, held by the tension like a microscopic specimen between two pieces of glass. Hammersham's stillness was that which immediately precedes swift and decisive action. And the man in the boiler suit, kneeling over the white plastic cone, was still because he was totally unaware that he had been discovered.

Then the instant was over. Hammersham took a long stride towards the intruder. His foot crunched on the stones and the man in the boiler suit heard him at last, turning and rising from his knees in one movement. The earphone fell out of his ear and dangled against his chest like a plastic medal.

He was about thirty years old with a college boy haircut and fashionable aviator-shaped glasses. He was handsome in the way people in film advertisements are handsome, and he had a suntan. He reminded me of one of the Beach Boys in the early sixties.

His mouth opened but he didn't get any words out.

Hammersham raised his hand and I knew immediately afterwards that he had intended nothing more than to grab the intruder by the shoulder. But as he did it I was convinced that he was going to hit him, and so was the man in the boiler suit.

He was younger and fitter and somebody had trained him. His hand shot up and he had grasped Hammersham's wrist before it got anywhere near him. That was his mistake. The circle of misunderstanding was complete. Someone had struck Hammersham on his own territory and he was furious. All the restraint of years of boardroom battles, where the only blows were words and figures in a cheque-book, dropped away from him very suddenly, and instead of one of the most influential people in Britain, he was just a man who has been attacked and is going to defend himself.

He lashed out with his other fist and caught the younger man a powerful unscientific blow on the chest. All this happened for me as though I was watching a film. It was totally unexpected and I did not realize, for a long moment, that I had any relation to what was going on at all. It was partly the fact that you simply do not think of yourself as having any influence on the lives of the great and powerful, but there was something else too. I had spent too much time writing about the things other people were doing and not enough doing things myself. That was going to change, and it was going to change more drastically than I could have imagined. But it hadn't changed yet.

I did nothing for about ten seconds. And then the man in the boiler suit was going over backwards, and taking Hammersham with him. He fell because he was tripped, as he staggered from Hammersham's blow, by the tracks which run around the edge of the roof of Amalgamated House. The tracks support a crane from which is lowered a six-foot box for the window-cleaners, and as I watched both men came down heavily on the rails and I heard a deep grunt of pain.

And then I began to move. It took me a very short time to get to the edge of the roof, but by the time I got there it was almost too late. They were locked together, struggling to rise from the wet metal, and inches away each of them knew that there were two hundred feet of tastefully tinted glass and a long drop to ten square yards of concrete solid with ornamental pebbles.

There was no finesse in what I did. I grasped both men by the collar and hauled them away from the drop. It was only a matter of feet, but it was enough. They tore apart, and the younger man swung around on me like a cat and smashed me hard across the face. It was not a particularly forceful blow, but it hurt, it bloodied my nose, it brought tears to my eyes and it gave him the moment he needed. He twisted away and took off across the gravel as if it had been a sprint track.

He had reached the fire-door almost before my eyes had cleared, but I can sprint too and I was up with him before he closed it, and would have had him. But then I turned to glance back at Hammersham, and when I did so I stopped dead. He was kneeling by the rails, trying to get up, and his face was grey, slate grey. I could hear the rasp of his breath from where I stood. I let go of the door and went over to him, fast.

2 Paper Chase

There were several nasty moments then, but there were some pills, and we got them out of his pocket and he swallowed them and finally we got down off the roof and into the deep-carpeted world of his office suite, and the secretary appeared. She was very calm and capable and I think she knew him better than he knew himself. She took over. All the right procedures were set in motion and all the right people called. The doctor appeared within three minutes, and I turned to go. I was in the hall when Hammersham's secretary caught up with me. She said: 'Would you say nothing about this to anyone, please? Lord Hammersham will be in contact.'

And that was that.

I got into the lift again and went down to the ground floor and left, and as I did so the sky opened and the rain began to hurl itself down. I turned my collar up around my neck and ran for the bus.

North Kensington is not a salubrious area at the best of times, and in that bleak, dripping winter it was at its worst. The streets were full of sodden rubbish and the dogs slunk into the doorways of boarded-up shops, waiting. The old people clustered together in the launderettes. At the end of my street the tower block rose into the rain like a giant tombstone. There was a trail of spray-paint across the door to my basement. When I opened the door it was like walking into a refrigerator. I went down the stairs fast and unlocked my flat.

I like the rooms I have down there. They have the right womb-like feel to them, and for some reason there is a light shaft that goes four storeys up to the roof. I have the bed beneath it, and when I lie there I can look straight up into the sky. Sometimes I can see the stars in daytime.

It's a very functional flat. There is no distinguishing where the office ends and the living space begins. The furniture is all junk and the communications equipment is all pretty good. The telephone on the desk might catch your eye. Instead of a hand-piece there are headphones and a mike. I tried the headsets the Post Office puts out and hated them. This way I talk and listen and type and record in comfort when I'm on the telephone. I spend quite a lot of time on the telephone. It's my job. Next to the phone is the tape deck and on shelves above that the amp and the tuner and the turntable and next to them all the tele-vision, on the filing cabinet. There's a little console on the wall by the bed, so I can turn them all on and off and change stations and things like that, without moving.

Around the bed are the bookshelves and next to them is the table with the copying machine and all the layout stuff. There is a big notice-board full of notices to remind me what I am supposed to be doing. There are several in-trays and out-trays. A door leads into a kitchen the size of a packet of cornflakes and another door leads into a bathroom about half that big.

There are no revolutionary posters on the walls. It's a one-person flat, and when I have women there they know it and try to change things and there's no space for that so after a while they usually go.

Now I lay back on the bed and put a disc on the turntable and fitted the headphones and looked up into the sky. I re-played the scene and replayed it again. I rubbed my fingers over the bruised flesh on my face. It didn't mean anything. I pulled together all the pieces I knew about Hammersham and Amalgamated National and took them apart again. They still didn't mean anything.

Later on I called some people, worked till nine, and listened to music till I slept. Everything turned itself off then. I built it that way.

The call came at eleven the next morning. It was the secretary. She said: 'Can you come in? Now?' and when I said yes she put the phone down.

I switched the lights out and locked the door and left.

Hammersham sat on the other side of a desk the size of an aircraft carrier. When I came in he stood up and we shook hands. He was fine. I was fine. There was silence for a moment.

'I'd like to thank you very much for what you did for me yesterday. I don't think it's putting it too strongly to say that you saved my life. I'm very grateful for that, you know.'

I said something in reply. I don't remember what.

'I wonder . . . would you be prepared to assist me further?' Pause. 'This time I'll be able to pay you some expenses.' He spoke quietly, unemphatically, and if you hadn't been listening for it you wouldn't have noticed the underlying note of urgency. He was accustomed to use his voice to command attention, and he did it effectively. I didn't stop him, so he went on. 'It'll involve a trip overseas. Could be a little difficult, could be very simple. You'd need to leave straight away. Could you do it?'

I let a small spotlight in my head play over the list of important things I had to do in the very near future. It didn't take long.

'Possibly,' I said. 'Where to and what for?'

Hammersham was silent again for a moment, then he got up and walked round to a small refrigerator in the wall beside his desk and said, 'Spot to drink?'

'I'll have a beer if you've got it.'

He poured me a beer and himself a whisky and sat down behind his desk again. He drank some of the whisky and I drank some of the beer and we were both satisfied. He settled back in his chair.

'We're speaking in confidence?' and he raised his eyebrows till I nodded. 'I remember driving down to the docks with my father just before the war,' he said, 'and watching the ships unloading the bales of paper from Scandinavia. I remember he turned to me and said, "That, my boy, is men's minds. *I* say what gets printed on that." '

He looked at me suddenly, and half smiled. 'You wouldn't have liked my father. Dare say he wouldn't have liked you.'

I smiled back at him. He was quite right, on both counts.

'At that time, newsprint cost nine pounds a tonne. In nineteen seventy-three it was ninety pounds a tonne. Last year it was one hundred and thirty pounds. This year it's one hundred and seventy pounds. I spend seventy million pounds a year on newsprint, and I can't go on doing that for long. There are those who say that newspapers are an outmoded way of conveying information, that it must all become a matter of electronic media, but I don't believe it. What I do believe is that newspapers won't survive if in addition to everything else they also have to compete for an increasingly costly resource like paper.

'You may know of Jim Wells. He's been my closest adviser for many years and we considered this question deeply a year or two back, and decided to attack the problem almost literally at the root. We decided to see if it was possible to make paper less scarce by making trees grow faster.'

Hammersham paused and I looked suitably startled and impressed. The idea was clearly his brainchild and he was proud of it. It *was* a good idea, actually. He steepled his fingers and looked wisely at me across the desk-top.

'I spent some of the war in the Far East, in the jungle, and if there's one thing that strikes you about the jungle it's the way it grows. I made inquiries about that. It seems it's not just that there is plenty of heat and rain in the tropics, it's the nature of the plants. They have a biological mechanism which enables them to concentrate the carbon dioxide in the air much more effectively than other plants, so photosynthesis occurs much faster and they grow faster. They call them plants of the C-4 variety.

'What Jim Wells and I asked ourselves was: would it be possible to do some genetic juggling with the pine trees from which paper is made so that some of these C-4 characteristics could be transferred to them? So we set up a small research project in New Zealand, to find out.'

'Why New Zealand?' I asked. 'They don't send us paper, do they?'

'No,' said Hammersham. 'It's too far away, though they do have some quite respectable forests which produce pulp and timber for Australasian consumption. But there were two factors which influenced that choice. One was their climate. Pine trees already grow about twice as fast there as in the Northern hemisphere because the winters are so mild. They grow all year round. The other reason was a man named Bill Hawk.'

'I think I've heard of him,' I said. 'I read his name in an article about the Green Revolution. Wasn't he one of the people connected with that strain of "super rice"?'

'Correct,' said Hammersham. 'He was. He's one of the most brilliant plant geneticists in the world and I happened to know he'd become interested in trees of late. I tracked him down and found he'd gone to live in New Zealand. He was working at their Department of Scientific and Industrial Research – they were on to something that appealed to him. So I made contact with him, told him what I was after, and offered him very generous research facilities to combine his own pursuits with mine. To cut a long story short, he accepted. I bought up an area of private pine forest at a place called Hinaki near the centre of the North Island, set up a research station, and Bill recruited a couple of other boffins to assist him.'

'How long ago was that?'

'Three years. Since then regular reports, steady work, no spectacular progress, until three weeks ago. Then they sent in a couple of pages which could mean a revolution for the newspaper industry. One of their *pinus radiata* specimens had started to grow four times as fast as a normal tree.'

'Inside or outside a lab?'

'Outside, that was the thing. It had been showing signs of unusual activity in the infra-red chamber they use to speed up the maturing of the seedlings. At first they put it down to some freak of those conditions, but six months ago they transplanted it and waited for it to settle down. It didn't. It just carried on reproducing cells at a fantastic rate. When they finally decided they were on to the real thing they sent us that report. And naturally we had to go and see for ourselves. We had to decide what to do next. We still do.'

'And both you and Jim Wells went out there?'

'No, only Jim. I had a deal on that I couldn't abandon. He couldn't get away immediately either. It wasn't until a week ago that he left. I haven't heard from him since.'

'Did you expect to?'

'Yes, I did. Jim and I work very closely together and since he left there have been at least half a dozen important decisions on which I've needed to consult him. We had an arrangement for him to ring daily. He hasn't phoned once.'

'Have you contacted Bill Hawk? Do you know if he's reached – where is it – Hinaki?'

'No idea. I can't phone them because Hinaki isn't on the phone. It's very remote, hard up against the mountains, and there's only an access road up to five miles away and then a track. They have a post box number in Rotorua, which is a town a considerable distance away. I've sent three telegrams and none of them has been collected.'

'The police?'

Hammersham looked at me thoughtfully and said, 'No, I haven't contacted them.'

There was a pause.

'Why is that?' I asked, at last.

Hammersham shifted in his chair. 'Because I'm in the middle of two very complex deals, and Jim Wells is vital to both of them. I won't go into details because they're nothing to do with this. But if word gets out to the people I'm dealing with that something has happened to Jim, well, at the least my timing will be badly thrown out and at worst I could sustain quite a lot of damage. That's why I haven't made an official request to the New Zealanders to look for Jim, and that's why I haven't sent one of my own staff. In an organization like this if you start sending search parties off, word spreads. Until I know for certain something is wrong I want to avoid that. Now it occurs to me that you might be the ideal solution. Your going need be known to no one here at all. It should excite no suspicion. If it's simply a failure of communications at the New Zealand end you can establish that. If Jim is . . . out of action . . . you can let me know directly and I can act accordingly, in my own time. And if he is in need of any assistance – I think you could render it. Are you prepared to give it a go?'

I drank the rest of my beer and put the glass down on top of the desk. 'You obviously believe this bugging attempt was something to do with your tree research or Jim Wells. Have you any notion of how they do connect up – who I'd be up against?'

He knew how to field this one, and I knew exactly the way he'd do it. I'd seen him on television. He leant forward across the desk and looked me straight in the eyes and said: 'I'll be quite honest with you (*a*) yes, I do think that, and (*b*) I have no actual evidence for doing so. If I were an American detective I'd say it was a hunch. It's a hunch I feel I ought to play, because Jim Wells is very close to me and if he is up against people like our friend on the roof, he'll need some help. Who they might be I don't know either. The only way to find out is to move into their territory. But be under no illusions. If I'm right, there could be some physical danger. All I can do is offer you reasonable remuneration and insure you. Does that put you off?'

It did, to be quite honest. But I wasn't going to tell Hammersham that. It would have pleased his father. I said: 'When do you want me to leave?'

'Splendid. Thank you very much.' He got up from behind his desk and came round and I stood up and we shook hands. All trace of the shocked and beaten man I had levered to his feet on the rooftop had gone. He was the executive again, the boss; and I was on the payroll, and that was that item of business disposed of for today.

'Would tonight be possible? Passport and all that in order?

Good. The only other person who need be involved is my secretary. She knows just what is going on and she'll provide you with all the information and expenses you need and a contract to sign. Needless to say, I'd like daily phoned or cabled reports on developments.' He walked me over towards the door and looked at me sincerely. 'Thank you again, old chap. And the best of luck.'

I walked through the door and into the outer office. It had started.

3 Eastern Promise

The 747 took off from Heathrow that afternoon, refuelled at Bahrain, and landed in Singapore some time during the next day.

I felt, as I always do when I fly, a brief, almost religious ecstasy for a short time after take-off. The world flees away beneath you, the planet begins to turn without you, and all the passions twenty thousand feet below shrink into ephemerality. You wonder how human beings can ever start wars.

Then I began to concentrate on consuming the small luxuries of first-class air travel, and memorizing the information in the slim dossier which Hammersham's secretary had compiled, and going to sleep. I woke as we landed to refuel and stared stonily out, half conscious, at the night and the fierce white lights breaking the darkness outside. Then I wrapped the blanket around myself and slept again.

This time I was on top of an immense white plastic cone and below me the streets seemed to be on another planet. Then I was sitting in the window-cleaners' gondola, floating gently down backwards and then forwards in the breeze, like a leaf from a tree. The man in the boiler suit was in there too, playing the accordion, and we both looked up to see Hammersham leaning over the edge of the roof waving good-bye to us with his cheque-book.

When I woke again we were flying above the South China Sea, and I looked down on enamelled blue dotted with the shiny green of small islands. As we came in to land I could see the sails of small boats.

Then Singapore was beneath us, very small and very green, and the 747 came down on what seemed to be a very short runway and there was the familiar bounce as the plane hit the ground again, and we were there. They opened the doors and drove the mobile steps up to the plane and we began to file out.

It was like stepping into an oven. It was as though the sky had been turned into a vast mirror overhead. It was like stepping on to another planet.

The first few hours in a completely foreign country can be like what the first few hours after birth would be like, if you were old enough to enjoy them. You *notice* everything, for one thing. And the air is like wine.

The green of the forest was like no green I had ever seen before, and it crowded in on the road into town as though it would swallow it. The roadside was bright with huge, crudely-coloured hoardings for Chinese films, and the bus, as it neared the city, began to plough through throngs of motor-scooters, motor-rickshaws, yellow taxis and bullock-carts, like a launch on a river filled with debris.

When I got down off the bus in the city, and just breathed in the smell of the East, I smiled. The whole thing was like a big present, an unexpected gift. I hadn't very closely analysed why I was on this trip, and I didn't intend to start. The whole thing had been arranged by chance, and I was content to leave it at that. What would happen at the other end I didn't know and was not going to consider yet either.

But here I was, on the very Land's End of the Eurasian continent, and before I left it for the island regions on someone else's mission, I was going to enjoy it. The wheels of profit and private enterprise had turned and this was the square I had landed on, and while I was here I would drift with the tide and pretend I had just been born.

I began to walk down the streets and to interpret the language of the air. Quite a lot of it was dried fish, piled in raffia baskets on the pavement and hanging in bunches around shop awnings. There was the smell of eastern spices as well, and garlic and joss sticks, and hot oil and curry, steaming rice, great pungent fruits like giant chestnuts, heaps of small green oranges and pineapples, piles of rubber, and petrol fumes.

Each street was overflowing with traffic, motors roaring, motor-horns shrieking ceaselessly. Any gaps in the sound-cover were filled by discordant Chinese pop songs and wailing Tamil dirges from a thousand transistor radios.

Each alley had a carnival atmosphere which I couldn't identify at first, because most were full of pretty nondescript buildings with dead paint peeling from grubby concrete and tatty shutters. Later I realized it was the washing slung out from every window on grey poles, like flags, drying stiff in the intense heat.

On either side of each street ran dark tunnels which were the pavements. They were separated from the roadway by deep monsoon drains and made dark by faded canvas awnings hanging from bamboo poles between the pillars which supported the overhanging upper storeys. Between the awnings and the open shop fronts the pavements were jammed with a mass of goods like some vast, eccentric Christmas party. There were baskets full of dried fish, baskets of ancient pickled eggs like lumps of coal, and chickens in little cages, hurricane lamps, speedboat engines, sieves, pans, electric mixers, huge urns full of oil, jars of pink sweets from Hong Kong, cheap mats, bales of cloth, tinned Peking Duck, tins of everything. Old men in grey singlets and pyjamas slept on piles of rubber, pulling at long mole-hairs, and children swung from cradles like chest expanders among the sharks' fins and birds' nests and oilskin umbrellas.

'Come in, sir, Jack, very good business, just in today, isn't it? Very nice hat, sir, very good business, come in and look around.'

I walked on, down street after street, drinking glass after glass of coconut milk, freshly-squeezed orange juice, mango juice, soya bean milk bought from little carts at every corner. I walked to Raffles Place, past the Post Office, into audio shops full of duty-free goods and air conditioning, like cool pools after the muggy street. I caught a bus up to Orchard Road and walked round C. K. Tang's Emporium and smelt the sandal-wood and looked at the ivory and silks and then I caught another bus. In its relative cool I let the shops glide by until I found myself in the middle of a huge empty field. The office blocks and monumental buildings and traffic were now a barely audible buzz and a blur at the edge of my view. The sky hung huge and deadly overhead.

Then I went out past the Hindu Temple, through the housing estates, to a hillside out of town, covered with the gods and monsters of Chinese and Western myth, in bright-painted concrete, a garden of tasteless delight donated by two brothers who had become millionaires on the profits of selling little pots of balm to put on mosquito bites. Small groups of teenagers stood before their ancient gods, thoughtful, dressed in their uniform of black flared pants, white shirts and belts with buckles printed with the legend 'James Bond a Go-Go'. They all wore sunglasses.

Down below, the harbour lay glassy in the afternoon sun, like a crumpled piece of silver cigarette paper. It was too bright to make out more than the black shapes of the craft anchored there, mostly still, the odd one moving in a slow lazy curve.

I went back into town and it was evening. I walked through Raffles Place and down Change Alley, Aladdin's Alley, full of seaweed arms and siren voices selling photograph albums and cameras and hunting jackets. I turned left and walked along the waterfront and past the Post Office and the Bank of Hong Kong and came to the sluggish chocolate creek that flows through the city. All along its left bank there are scores of tiny restaurants. Each one consists of a charcoal brazier, a battered cupboard full of food, a big rounded metal dish on the brazier and an ancient table covered with a faded plastic cloth. There are chairs round the tables that look as though they were specially designed for Methodist meeting halls. There is Chinese, Malay, Indonesian and Indian food and nearly all of it is cheap and good. It comes on cracked plates heaped with fluffy rice, together with pale Chinese tea, and there is a constant cloud of steam around the cooking, and a white blaze of Tilley lanterns, and the place was noisy and busy and I liked it.

I ate a lot and watched the creek flow slowly past and

thought that once it had flowed through a swamp and jungle down to a silent, empty sea. I drank a lot of tea.

When it was time I walked away from there and through the crowded streets until I reached the airline office, and checked that the plane was leaving that night at the time it was supposed to be leaving. Yes, it was, but there was no bus to the airport at the right time, for some reason. The airline had organized taxis. There would be one outside now, if I was ready.

I went outside and sure enough, the taxi was there, and the driver was ready and I was the only passenger who had not yet been ferried out. I got in and it was very pleasant to sink back in a comfortable seat and watch the city run by outside the window like a film running backwards. I was tired now, as passive as a slightly tipsy passenger on a charabanc outing coming home at the end of the day, cheerful, smiling and drifting off to sleep.

I was out here at someone else's bidding, to oil the wheels of a system I didn't entirely believe in, and what the hell, I had enjoyed myself. I looked out of the window at the night markets, at the piled stalls and the crowds and began to drift into a doze.

When I woke up again the crowds and the lights had gone and outside the darkness had flooded over the world and there was nothing to stop it. With frightening suddenness all the deep childhood fears of being alone and unprotected in an alien darkness, in a strange and friendless city, flooded in on me and the night chill of the tropics struck me at the same time. I tried to snap out of it, but I couldn't. I was frightened and, though it seemed irrational, I was sure that there was something wrong. I looked at my watch. We should have been at the airport ten minutes ago.

I leant over to the driver. 'We should have reached the airport by now,' I said. He muttered something I didn't catch, without turning to face me. I sank back in the seat. Where the hell were we? Was I being hijacked? Was this the road to the airport?

Then we passed a lighted sign and as we passed it the words struck some chord in my mind and I remembered where I had seen them before. Did I still have it? I fumbled in my pocket and found that I did. It was a little booklet put out by the Singapore Chamber of Commerce, listing shops of interest, and in the middle of it was an outline map of the island. It showed the airport and it showed the Shining Bag Crocodile Farm and Workshop. The airport was in one direction from the city and the Shining Bag shop was in the other direction. The sign I had just seen had read 'The Shining Bag Crocodile Farm'.

I was being hijacked.

I looked at the doors and they were perfectly ordinary doors. No one had removed the inside handles, the way they do in the movies. But the taxi was going far too fast to consider turning one of those handles and opening the door and jumping out. I was stuck here until the taxi stopped.

It was then that I began to think about Singapore in an entirely different way. I remembered little facts that I had forgotten, like its proximity to the opium-producing areas of the East and the fact that it was the base for some of the biggest criminal operators in the Orient and the fact that it has quite enough unemployed young people to man a Mafia-style army several times over.

Outside there were no lights at all now, just the blackness of the jungle.

I looked at the back of the driver's head. He had a white shirt and greased black hair. It didn't tell me anything. Very quickly I leant right over the front seat, reached for the key, turned it and pulled it out of the lock. The engine died and the car sped on silently, slowing.

In that same instant the driver had my wrist. That saved me, I think. His other hand had to stay on the wheel and his knife was behind the sunshield. He didn't get to it until I had twisted out of his grasp, the wrist cracking as though a bone had snapped.

Then it was very close. The knife flashed in the dark, slicing through my jacket, as I wrenched at the handle of the door. It flashed again and the door was open, and again, and I was falling. The car rushed on past me, and I hit the road hard. The breath was knocked out of me as I fell but I saw what was behind me, and I knew that I had lost.

The taxi-driver had just been the hospital porter. The surgeons were coming up behind, on scooters, without lights.

They had been close all the time and when they heard the engine die they'd closed in. When I hit the ground they almost ran me over, and for an instant I looked straight up into their faces, into the goggled eyes, like the eyes of giant insects.

Then I was rolling away from them across the road, and the ground gave way beneath me and became a ditch and my feet were sliding about in the mud at the bottom and my hands were tearing out lumps of grass on the farther side and I was on my hands and knees and hauling myself up and out. Then the ground was firm again and dead vegetation snapped and broke beneath my feet and I was running in great heart-bursting strides across a clearing, and around me there was a circle of thatch huts, on stilts, and around them was the forest, like a wall. I heard behind me, under the roar of my own sobbing breath, the sound of running feet on a wooden bridge, and then in front of me there was a set of steps leading up to one of the huts and I leapt up them and through the doorway and inside. The whole building shuddered as I entered and the thatch whispered to itself uneasily. And then everything was silent again. Too silent.

The village was dead. Every hut was empty, every doorway was black, and there were no animals or tended gardens. There was no one here at all and there had been no one here for some time. Why?

I peered out into the blackness, straining to see a shadow move, trying to still my own breath to hear a sound. Nothing. Where the hell were they?

Suddenly I was sure. They had crept around the village and had got into this hut and were moving towards me through the darkness somewhere behind me. A spasm of fear shot through me like an electric shock and I had to freeze and force myself to remain still until the panic had passed. There was no way they could have done that without my hearing. They were out there somewhere and if I looked hard enough I would see them before they saw me. Because they had to move.

The sky was pale overhead, moonless, but glowing yellow with the lights of the city. The city seemed very far away. I still couldn't see anything.

Then I caught them, sound and vision together; a shadow on the steps of the fourth hut to my right, and the creak of wood. A second shadow joined the first. There was nothing for a moment, and then they passed on to the next hut. This time I saw what they were doing; one searched, one stayed outside to spot me if I made a break from somewhere else. They were sensible, they were efficient, and in the next two minutes they would find me. I caught a gleam of steel in their hands as they left the first hut. And no one was going to come back and interrupt them. I had it now – the reason why the village was dead. They had taken all the people away to decant them into tower blocks, because tower blocks, in Singapore, are still progress, and progress is still what matters. I remembered reading about Singapore's progressive rehousing policies in a news magazine, and about the bulldozers, coming soon, to clear away the debris of a past that had been condemned. And I knew that if I did not move, I would be part of that debris, because they would have me. I had to move. And I could not.

It was a paralysis of will; I didn't feel so much frightened as paralysed, as I watched while the two figures searched one hut and then another and then another. Just keep still, stay silent, and everything will be all right, part of me said. Don't let them see you, whatever you do. A sergeant-major in my head was screaming at me to act and I couldn't do it, and his mouth was opening and closing and no sound was coming out. Still.

They were in the next hut to mine. I could hear them now; I could hear a blade rip through thatch and a sharp indrawn breath of anger.

Now. I had to make a break now, while they were occupied. Another second and it would be too late. Suddenly the paralysis broke, and it was too late. They had finished the next hut and they were coming up the steps of mine and I was still there. I stepped back into the darkness.

The floor creaked.

They were up the steps in an instant, and there was no hope of rushing past them; I stumbled back into the interior and they came through the door, half-crouched, knives ready, trying to see me.

I was still again. There was perhaps a yard between us. Behind me I was conscious of the palm-thatched wall, inches away. No exit.

Then they picked me out, both together, and leapt. I threw myself backwards, pointlessly, without plan, without hope. I hit the palm thatch. Now they would have me, pinned against the wall, like an insect. I went straight through.

I didn't know what was happening for the seconds of the fall. I was sure they had hit me, but they hadn't. I had thrown myself backwards at the palm-thatched wall and it had simply given way. The hut was old and abandoned and rotten, it had simply given way.

Then I was on my feet and running. The clearing was gone and the ditch was coming up in front of me. There was no time to think, I just jumped. Behind me I could hear a confused crashing and breaking of wood and two voices. I didn't listen to them. The taxi-driver was still in his cab, waiting, no doubt, to be paid. He looked up, open-mouthed, as I landed on the roadway. But I wasn't taking any notice of him; it was the scooters which interested me.

I was still running when I reached them and I barely stopped. They were facing the wrong way so I grabbed the handlebars of the nearest and heaved it round and off its stand in one movement. I could hear the taxi door opening and the shouting growing nearer. They must have left the key in, they must.

They had. I saw it as I ran, wheeling the scooter alongside me, and when I saw it I jumped astride and, kicking it along with my feet, twisted savagely at the key. The engine started.

I didn't look behind but I knew they were within feet of me. I felt a hand grab at my jacket and heard it tear. The little engine on the machine screamed and whined shrilly, but it was enough. The footsteps faded in to the distance and I was away.

Behind me I heard the taxi start and it drowned out the noise of the second scooter. I knew the taxi had to turn but the scooter could be after me in a matter of seconds. Whether I would beat them I didn't know and I didn't care. I was out of that damned graveyard, and that was enough.

They didn't pursue me. We had stopped too near an inhabited area, I think, and it was only a matter of minutes before the roadway was lit again and there were houses and traffic. They weren't going to risk it a second time.

As I rode I asked myself what I was going to do, and the answer was that when I got to the airport I would ignore the flight on to Sydney and Auckland, and get straight on the next one back to Heathrow. I wasn't cut out for this sort of thing.

As soon as I had decided this I felt a warm glow of relief. I had been a fool to allow myself to be talked into this in the first place. I would be an even bigger fool if I didn't get out before it was too late.

When I got to the airport I took my passport and ticket out of the wallet I kept under my shirt, and walked over to the ticket counter for my airline. When I got there the woman took the ticket and before I could explain what I wanted she looked anxiously at her watch and said, 'You should just about make it. Your case is already aboard. I'll call them and tell them you're coming.' And she picked up the telephone beside her. I opened my mouth to speak but a call on the Tannoy system drowned my words. The ticket girl looked up anxiously from the phone, saw I was still there, and waved me on. I opened my mouth again and then closed it. I smiled at her and began to walk towards the passenger exit.

4 Evasive Action

I got across the tarmac and up the steps and down the length of the plane with every appearance of normality, and as I did so I mechanically took off my jacket and folded it so that the two rents did not show, because such things are not suitable for the comfortable, protected world of airline passengers; and the hostess got me to my seat and made sure I was strapped in, and we began to taxi down the runway. Then the reaction started. As the plane heaved itself into the air and the island began to disappear into the darkness below, I gripped the arm-rests and sat staring rigidly in front of me while the short, vivid film of what had just happened was run forwards and backwards through my mind, over and over again. The hijack. The knife in the car. Hitting the road. The ditch. And waiting, while the shadows closed in. When I didn't know what to do . . . and waiting . . .

The reaction lasted some time, and it was only broken down, bit by bit, as the hostesses brought along trays and drinks and food and magazines and headphones. There were enough distractions to force me back into the present, and by the time I had eaten and drunk three cans of Australian lager, the film in my head was beginning to look like an old print, the colour was fading, and I was almost able to stop it at will. I was on the plane and the plane was going to New Zealand, but that didn't necessarily mean I had to follow through; I could get off at Sydney and go home. I *wanted* to get off at Sydney and go home. The only reason for not doing so was that there was a job to do and I had undertaken to do it. I don't like giving jobs up half-way through. On the other hand no one had ever tried killing me half-way through a job before.

We had been very foolish, both Hammersham and I. If we believed that the people doing the bugging were the people interfering with Jim Wells twelve thousand miles away, we ought to have concluded that they wouldn't give up just because we'd startled them. If they had instituted surveillance, surveillance would continue. Obviously it had. I'd taken no precautions when I'd left Amalgamated House and gone home to pick up my passport. I'd just walked out into the street, caught my bus, and ridden off. Whoever had been watching Hammersham's office had seen me there and on the roof. It would have been only reasonable to check whether I was involved, even if they hadn't heard a word of what Hammersham had said. It was just a matter of time before I came out. And it must have been the simplest thing in the world to follow me home, hang around to see whether I went any place, and then tail me to Heathrow when I did. And when I was there it would not have been difficult to discover which flight I was taking and where it was going. A cable to the first port of call, with full description, and hey presto, a ninety per cent chance of eliminating further enquiries. Correction. A ninety-nine per cent chance.

From now on I was going to keep my head down. So who were they? One of them appeared to be an American. That didn't really mean anything. It could be an organization which happened to employ an American. It needn't necessarily be an American organization. But if it was an American organization there was one that sprang immediately to mind. They were supposed to be on our side, weren't they? I began to think hard about just how you go about avoiding the attentions of people like that. It wasn't going to be easy. For a start they could pick me up at Mangere Airport without any difficulty at all. At airports you have to queue up to get your passport stamped and your luggage checked and when you are standing in queues people holding your photograph can look up and say 'Ah, there he is.'

I pursed my lips and looked out of the window. There had to be a way round that sort of situation. I constructed a scenario of what was likely to happen at the airport and the options I would have then. I made lists of them and crossed them out one by one. When I'd done that I had a course of action and it may not have been the best one, but it was the best one I could think of and just having it made me feel better.

I would take the bus from the airport to the city. You can't shake pursuers on a bus but they can't do much to you either. When I got off the bus in the terminal I would try to lose them in the city streets. That might be difficult but it would certainly be easier than at the airport. When I thought I had lost them in the city streets I would try to come up on them unawares. The venue for that part of the operation would be the Embassy Hotel.

I chose the Embassy Hotel because Hammersham's secretary had booked me in there. If these people were efficient enough to find me in Singapore they were efficient enough to find me at the Embassy Hotel. If they lost me on the way from the airport they would come looking for me there. I would be waiting for them.

After this decision was made, I slept.

After Sydney, when I woke, it was day, and beneath us was the Tasman Sea and they served us an airline breakfast and the sky was pure blue as far as the eye could see. And then there was a smudge of land down there and the plane was coming in over a rich royal blue harbour snaking around green headlands covered in white houses with red roofs, and we landed. My work had begun.

I did what I had planned to do at the airport, and because I had planned to do it it seemed right, and it gave me confidence. When I got out of the terminal building and on to the bus the weather was superb and the air was warm, without the cloying dampness of South East Asia, and I felt like singing. I can't sing, so I didn't, but I felt like it. The country looked clean and bright and new, and slightly like Toyland. It looked like England after a spring-clean. All the houses seemed to be made of wood and they all had roofs made of painted corrugated iron.

We made it to the bus terminal, which was large and dimly lit like bus terminals usually are, and I stepped down off the bus with my little suitcase and scanned the faces in the crowd just in case there was one with a scar and a fedora hat, but there wasn't. I walked out of the bus terminal into the street, which was on a hill. The buildings were big, not perhaps quite as big as they are in British cities, but all designed by the same lousy architects for the same lousy patrons. The shops were full of the usual goods and only the advertisements had the ephemeral charm of unfamiliarity.

I got to the doors of the biggest department store on the street and went through them. As usual, the ground floor was full of cosmetics and perfumes and I felt as conspicuous as a hole in a plate-glass window. I went to the lift and got in and rode to the third floor, got out, walked into the next-door lift, and rode down to the second floor. There were other people in that lift but as they had all been at the top of the shop when I arrived I assumed them innocent until proved guilty. I got out on the second floor and walked over to the emergency exit and down the fire-stairs to the street. There wasn't anybody on the fire-stairs.

It wasn't the same street as the one I had left, but it did have another department store and I played the same game again, with different floors. Then I found myself in Queen Street, the main street, which is also on a hill, and a bus pulled up alongside me and I jumped on and went with it up the hill.

I found out later that after the British had bought the site of Auckland city from the native Maori owners for fifty blankets, a bag of sugar and a miscellany of items including twenty pairs of trousers, they employed a surveyor who was too fond of the bottle to lay out a plan for the city. He did the job on the assumption that the city was dead flat (it being easier that way, I suppose), ignoring the fact that it consists of hundreds of extinct volcanic cones. The nice part about the story is that the settlers, being British too, followed his plans to the letter, and for years had to cross Queen Street on bridges because he had placed it in the middle of a small ravine.

Queen Street runs down to the harbour, and the bus I took was going the other way, up the hill, away from the smart shops and hotels and up to a tatty area full of empty shops and clip joints and strip shows, from which a fine view of the city could be obtained. I obtained it and changed buses and rode around for perhaps half an hour. On the way I stopped long enough to buy a city map and found out where the Embassy Hotel was. Then I got out to the wrong side of the city and sat in a bus shelter for a while and watched people ride by on bicycles and in very old cars, and decided if anybody was still on to me they were being subtler than their previous behaviour made likely. Nobody joined me in the bus shelter and finally the bus arrived and I was back in the city again, in the streets behind Queen Street. I got off the bus and walked a little way until I was right behind the Embassy Hotel. The back looked just the way you expect the backs of big, expensive hotels to look: awful. There were ancient dustbins full of kitchen refuse and squashed cabbage leaves on the asphalt and a tall, bleak wall. I found the fire-escape behind the hotel and a fire-door at ground level, and a back door which was unlocked.

I had a story ready for anyone who asked me, but I didn't need it. I walked through a pretty dim and dirty corridor, through a set of swing doors and into a cleaner one, past the hotel kitchen. Then there was an assortment of doors to choose from and I tried three that were locked or opened on to empty cupboards before I found the one that led to the lobby. I took a quick survey of the layout and closed the door again.

It would need time, I knew that much. It would be a matter of watching the people coming and going and picking out the ones who waited and eliminating the ones who had a good reason for waiting. I knew I probably wouldn't be able to get the precise individual, but if I had two or three possibles engraved on my memory, when I came across them again, I would know. And that might matter a lot.

I went over the layout of the lobby again and made my decision. Then I opened the door and slipped quietly through. There was a massive pillar with tiny mosaic tiles in slate-grey and gold stuck to it. Around the base was a small tropical jungle. It made a perfectly acceptable hiding-place. The only other thing between the pillar and the wall was a fire hose on a reel, and if anyone came to grab that I would be having very bad luck indeed.

I was to the right of the main entrance, and I could see the crowd going up and down Queen Street too, through the glass walls around the automatic doors. The reception desk was about seven or eight yards from me. The lobby was fairly large, and seats for people waiting about were arranged around small circular tables which were too near the ground to be useful for anything except kicking over.

It was an expensive hotel and the lobby was decorated and furnished tastefully and without feeling. It had the regulation expensive carpet and the girls at the desk were as classy as clothes and make-up could make them. There were quite a number of people coming and going, most of them middle-aged, many of them Americans, and all of them easy to eliminate. Half an hour went by. Three-quarters. Fifty minutes. I kept looking more and more frequently at my watch to see how much time had passed, and wondering if I had outsmarted myself and my first move was going to be an overelaborate flop. Then I saw him. I recognized him immediately, strangely enough, though I hadn't seen him before and he didn't even come into the lobby at first. I caught sight of him just after he stepped out of a car and on to the footpath. It was a large car, I think, but I wasn't taking much notice until I saw the man and the car had pulled away. When he was on the footpath he walked briskly past the lobby and gave it a long, searching glance and then he went out of my field of vision for perhaps four minutes. After four minutes he came back at the same steady pace, walked through the automatic doors and up to the desk. He passed within a few feet of me and as he did so I felt as though a magnet had gone past me. I almost stepped out from behind the pillar and went up to him. It must have been jet-lag.

He was a tall man, about my own height, which is an inch or

two over six feet; he was thin and wore a well-cut suit and he
was nearer forty than thirty-five. Maybe his bearing was
purposeful but that didn't register. It was his face that did it:
especially the eyes. There was an opportunity to see them close,
once, later, and they were like the eyes of a reptile when it is
about to take its prey. Fear sat on that man's back like a passenger, and it almost drew me to him.

At the reception desk I heard my own name among the discreet murmur. I felt as though the potted plants would wilt in
front of me and the pillar crumble.

But nothing happened. The receptionist shook her head, and
the man said something and went to sit at the table in front of
my pillar. The only other detail that afforded me was that his
suit was blue-grey and that it was a tropical-weight suit. He lit
a cheroot and sat back to wait. He was twenty inches from
what he was waiting for.

I breathed deep and quietly and got ready to make a swift,
discreet exit the way I had come in. I had won. I had been very
lucky, and my gamble had paid off. It now remained to get
away with it.

Then I heard a swift intake of breath, twenty inches away,
and my heart stopped. Nothing happened. I heard the slight
squeak of leather as the man in the blue tropical suit got out
of the chair, and I turned in time to see him walk over to the
other side of the lobby, near the lift, and turn his back on the
reception desk, buying a newspaper at the gift counter near the
window.

There were only three other people in the lobby; two of them
were a husband and wife in their middle sixties and they were
walking out. The third was a man with a head covered with
tight black curls, standing at the reception desk, filling in a
form. The receptionist handed him a key and said, 'That's two
doors along from his room, sir. As soon as he does arrive I'll
phone you and let you know.' The man walked over to the lift
and got in and I heard him say 'Sixth' to the liftman. Then the
doors closed and he disappeared.

The man in the blue tropical suit glanced at the lift indicator, saw where it stopped, and stepped into the next lift. I didn't hear him say where he wanted to go but I watched the lift indicator too, and it stopped at the sixth.

I did what I had intended to originally and went out the way I had come in. I got into the back alley and breathed in its undistinguished air with unalloyed relief. Unalloyed, that is, except for one thing. I had to find out what was going on on the sixth floor.

I had to know just how many people were chasing me. And how friendly they were with each other.

This time I took the fire-escape. It didn't take long: but when I got to the sixth floor I found what I should have anticipated – the fire-door only opened from the inside and nobody had been careless with it. I went down to the fifth floor and nobody had been careless there either. I went up again past the sixth to the seventh and this time somebody had been careless. I inserted my fingers through the crack and pulled the door open. No trouble at all. I was in the corridor.

It was thickly carpeted and empty and I walked round it until I found the lift; I pushed the down button, waited, and held my breath while the doors opened in case there was someone in there I didn't want to see. There wasn't. It was empty, and it took me down to the sixth floor and when the doors opened for the second time I held my breath again, this time with more reason.

The man in the tropical suit was in the corridor. He'd just come out of one of the rooms. He'd heard the lift too and he wasn't wasting any time. I stepped away round the corner of the corridor and when I stepped back it was empty and the lift was still there. My pursuer had left by the fire-escape. I didn't know that but I guessed it and I felt pretty certain he'd been up to something which made him unwilling to go out of the Embassy Hotel the way guests normally do.

It wasn't long before I found out what. Just long enough for me to take a turn around the corridors of the sixth floor and walk twice past the door my friend had come out of. He hadn't closed it.

The third time round I knocked and prepared to run like hell.

There was no answer. I knocked again and said, 'Room service, sir' but there still wasn't any answer, so before I could have second thoughts about it, I grabbed the door-handle and pushed the door open.

It would have been nice to stay at the Embassy Hotel. The rooms were well furnished and so on, as one might expect, but the view was something really spectacular, and the windows, which were very large, made the most of it. The whole of Auckland Harbour was spread out below, complete with green shores, great ships, the billowing sails of yachts, and, in the distance, the cone of an island volcano. The city was sprinkled around the harbour like hundreds and thousands of sweets on green icing. The sky was a perfect lapis blue and the sun like the sun in all the best pictures.

The man with the tight curls wasn't looking at the view. The view wasn't any good to him at all. He was dead.

5 Time Out

He was slumped, half sitting by the curtains, his head down on his chest, eyes closed. His face was red, full of broken blood vessels, and the mouth was small, with thin red lips.

His toupee had come adrift and hung over one eyebrow as though he had been scalped, and it was that which convinced me he was dead because it reminded me somehow of a flag of surrender. He looked ugly and pathetic and I didn't want to go anywhere near him, and I knew I had to. I had to find out who he was and why he wanted me and I had to do it fast. Every minute I spent in here I was exposing myself to the very people I wanted to avoid, and if I needed any reminding why I wanted to avoid them, the man with the bulging eyes was quite enough. But I couldn't bring myself to go near him.

I looked round the room for a diversion, and I found one. An open suitcase lay on the bed. I pounced on it like a morsel of food and began sifting through the contents. By the time I was half-way through I knew I was being a fool. I was up against professionals, and professionals, when they want to hide things, hide them so amateurs like me can't find them. All the clothes in the case were new or newish; they all had local manufacturers' labels. There was a bush shirt and a pair of muddy walking boots in a plastic bag, two heavy jerseys and a shaving kit with the usual shaving things in it, and a transistor radio which I found was perfectly innocent. I was wasting my time.

There was no false bottom in the suitcase and there was nothing underneath it except a local newspaper. I picked it up and there was nothing underneath that either. I breathed deep and looked back at the body.

It was then somebody knocked at the door.

Doors are funny things. There may not be much to them, but they create worlds. When you shut the door to your own home at night, you've created a world, you've shut out a dimension.

Whoever knocked at that door opened a new dimension for me at that time. Super-terror. If I had been sure who it was I would have been able to deal with it. If I had been sure it was the man in the tropical suit I would almost have been able to deal with it. Not knowing, I was super-terrified.

The room suddenly became very small. If they'd been asking me to rent it I'd have laughed at them. There was a bathroom by the door. It was the size of a can of beans. There was a wardrobe. A half can of beans. And I didn't like the idea of dying in a wardrobe.

And outside the window the hotel dropped six storeys into that view. They saved the fire-escape for the crummy side of the building.

The only way out was the door.

My eyes focused on the door and fixed themselves on the chunky, matt-chrome, cone-shaped handle with a button in the middle for the keyhole, which is favoured in hotels that want to look like hotels in America. Outside, a hand closed round it and someone began to turn it, very slowly.

I did not know whether it was locked.

The cone turned smoothly in its little orbit, and my internal organs went round with it. Then it reached the end of its appointed round and stopped. There was a tiny movement of the whole door as someone pressed it gently.

It didn't open.

My internal organs went back round to their original positions and I listened. I didn't hear anything. Thick carpets have many advantages but hearing whether people have walked away down hotel corridors is not one of them.

Whoever had come to visit might be outside. Or he might not. There was only one way to find out.

I brought myself under control, gripped the newspaper I had picked up as if it had been a weapon of some sort that would actually be of some value to me if I were attacked, and took one long stride to the door. I took the handle, pressed the lock-button, and pulled it open.

There was no one outside.

I leapt across the corridor and hit the opposite wall. I whirled round.

The corridor was empty. The door swung closed behind me and I turned and began to walk briskly in the direction of the fire-door. I had to turn two corners before I was in its vicinity and both of them were difficult. When I turned the first one, two things happened. On the other side of the building the lift arrived and I heard the doors open, and four yards ahead of me a figure stepped out of his room.

I kept going. It wasn't the man in the tropical suit. That didn't mean a thing. I kept going. It wasn't a wide corridor, for all the thickness of the carpets, and he seemed to fill it. When we came alongside each other we both half-turned sideways, and murmured a ritual acknowledgement. If it was to happen here, this was the moment. It didn't. We passed and he was gone. I was alone in the corridor again and round the second corner and in front of the fire-door and pressing on the release-bar and out – out into the open again.

The fire-door shut itself loudly behind me, and I was alone on the fire-escape. I looked down through the criss-cross metal slats of the steps. No one. I started down, three steps at a time, the metal ringing under my feet and the alley walls closing in above me.

Just as I reached the alley, two men came out of the rear exit of the hotel carrying dustbins. One of them shouted something. I didn't turn. I jumped the last three steps on to the asphalt and headed for the eastern end of the alley. There were no footsteps after me. I reached a shopping street and the crowd closed over me like holy water.

A bus slowed for a traffic light and I jumped aboard and walked down into the dim interior, breathing in the familiar smell of worn leather and bus tickets, like incense. I was out.

When I reached the end of the bus and settled into a red

plastic seat – I remembered the newspaper. I was still holding it. I folded it up and put it away.

I rode on the bus for perhaps forty minutes, thinking out what I should do, and at the end of that time I'd remembered the names of three people I'd once known who'd said they lived in or came from Auckland, and I decided if ever I needed them, now was the time.

I got off the bus and took a handful of change into a call box and after half an hour I struck lucky. I took another bus and walked a little, and by late afternoon I was sitting on a wooden porch outside an old house in the part of the city where university students and poor people live.

As slums go, it wasn't in the same league as North Kensington, and it wasn't only because the air was soft and warm. All the houses were separate one-storey boxes in their own quarter-acres; they were squat, inelegant, wooden affairs with deep porches, the odd Gothic turret and big, steeply sloping roofs made of corrugated iron. The roofs were all painted maroon or red and the paint on the walls was faded until it couldn't remember what colour it was supposed to be. Strips of it curled thoughtfully away from the grey wood underneath, like whiskers.

All the lawns were bald, and there were motor-bike parts, old milk crates and sleeping cats where flower beds had once been. There were more cats stretched out asleep on the warm asphalt pavement, and in the windows. All the windows were tall and ugly, their sashes stuck together by innumerable coats of paint applied by hopeful amateurs. Resigned curtains drooped from spavined curtain wires.

The girl's name was Wendy, and she had long dark hair and big eyes and long suntanned legs. She'd looked pale and out of place when I'd seen her in London; now she was studying something at the university and she was back under her native sun, and that night they were having a party. She was dressed for the occasion in a teeshirt and jeans cut down to an extent I wouldn't have believed possible. She smiled a lot.

Inside the house the rooms were all unnaturally tall, papered with Edwardian wallpaper that wasn't a trendy reproduction, and filled with huge ugly Salvation Army wardrobes and lots of beds and home-made desks and sleeping-bags and books. There was an ancient cracked telephone and I sat beside it while Wendy and her friends got a meal ready, and dialled five numbers one after the other.

The first time was to the hotel where Wells had stayed when he'd arrived in Auckland. They told me he had checked out when he'd been expected to check out, on the morning he was due to go up to Hinaki, and he hadn't come back. He hadn't been expected back.

The second, third and fourth calls were to the big car-hire firms. Finally I found the firm where Jim had hired the car he needed to get to Hinaki. He'd hired it on the day he'd checked out of his hotel. Had he brought it back?

Yes, sir, he'd brought it back within the week. I digested this information. So if anything had happened to Jim Wells it hadn't happened at Hinaki. Which meant? I said to the girl: 'The car wasn't damaged or anything? There weren't any problems with it?'

No, sir, said the girl. Americans always seem to take good care of their cars.

Jim Wells wasn't an American. I described him to her.

No, the man who brought tthe car back didn't look like that at all. No, sir, the girl who originally checked it out wasn't here today. She'd be in on Thursday.

The fifth call was a collect cable to Hammersham.

Then we had supper.

The meal consisted of tinned fish and boiled potatoes and when we finished it we sat out on the porch drinking beer and waiting for people to turn up for the party. We could see the neighbours coming back from work or classes to start mending their cars. They padded in and out of their houses in their bare feet, carrying tools and car parts and cans of beer and calling to one another while the sun went down.

Wendy's friends went indoors to prepare things for the party and she and I sat back against the cracking paint of the wall, in that pleasant state before leaning against someone else's shoulder can be taken for granted, and she greeted her friends as they arrived without bothering to get up.

The sun sank lower and finally disappeared, leaving behind a salmon pink blaze streaked with midnight blue clouds, and the house filled up with people and they overflowed on to the porch and flagons of beer and plates of cheese dip and biscuits and sandwiches went their appointed rounds and were piled up, empty, in unlikely places.

I ate and drank and answered questions and listened with pleasure to the broad, soft accents while big, rugby-playing blokes called Dave and Bruce and Barry talked about their lives in distant tussock-farms and in little country towns where the social calendar revolved gently around race meetings and the seasons. We listened to the pop music we had all heard years before, when we were in a different age, and joined in the verses and the beer went down and the evening faded into night. Somebody heard me saying I was going down near Rotorua to see somebody about something and he said he was driving that way tomorrow and did I want a lift? I said yes.

Gradually the party began to slow and people began saying good-bye and headlights lit up the fences and ancient motors began to turn over. The house emptied until there were only half a dozen extras who had decided to stay the night, and people improvised with sleeping-bags and spare blankets, and couples disappeared, and Wendy and I stayed out on the porch and gathered a pile of bedding around ourselves and, after a while, we slept.

The Holden Estate pulled up outside at 8.30 next morning and Robert McIntosh leant on the horn for a minute or two until we all knew the night had ended and the earth had turned itself around once more. Then he came in to encourage us about breakfast, and there was a considerable amount of stumbling over sleeping bodies and finding bits of bread and half a pound of bacon and a few eggs; and then we sat around eating and washing the food down with strong coffee, and then it was time to go. Wendy and I wrote down telephone numbers and addresses and exchanged a few words about this and that, and she smiled at me in a way I would remember, and that was about it. I was sitting in the front seat of the Holden and she was waving and I was waving and Bob pulled the car out of the little street and into the traffic, and she was gone.

6 Volcanic Plateau

The roads in town were full of the morning traffic, so it took a little time to get to the motorway. Neither of us had much to say until we did. It was a time for not saying anything much.

Then we went round a looped ramp and down and into the valley of the motorway and all my sins of omission and commission rose up before me in a Cinerama technicolour as Bob put his foot down and explained to me just what could be got out of even something like a Holden if you knew how to drive it. I concentrated on keeping the muscles of my face straight, and tightened my safety belt until it hurt, to discourage me from climbing into the back seat and putting my arms over my head. I looked keenly out of the window.

Driving south through London is like driving through the bleached bones of a dinosaur. It looks like a dead city, and the endless rows of mass-produced terraced houses its ruins. Driving south through Auckland is more like travelling through a giant fungoid culture. The neat new wooden bungalows and quarter-acres go on and on, reproducing themselves as tentacles of red and grey surging along the motorway as if it were a source of food.

At last we broke free. The road roared straight on through a fat, prosperous, green countryside full of milking sheds and freshly painted dairy factories with shining chrome Anchor milk trucks outside, and sleek cows grazing behind meticulously-kept fences.

'Half Ocean Island been topdressed over that lot,' said Bob, dividing his attention for a moment between trying to overtake an MG and looking critically at the farms we passed. 'Superphosphate fertilizer. Some very prosperous cow cockies round here. 'Course it's been settled for a long time. Good hundred years . . . You should come down and see us in the Rangitiki some time. That's a bit more like it.' And he told me all about it, and I listened and felt the sun's warmth on the roof and opened the window and felt the cool fresh air flow over my face. It smelt good. On our right the Waikato River appeared at intervals, broad, smooth and brown. Once the British had sent gunboats down it, between banks solid with forest, to do battle with the Maoris in their immense earthworked villages. Some of the mounds were still there, Bob said. And one of the gunboats was used as a memorial for the real war, the one they fought twelve thousand miles from here, after Sarajevo.

We stopped in Hamilton, a biggish town beside the river with a wide, bland main street full of sun and farmers' wives, and we drank a strawberry milkshake apiece, through straws, out of aluminium tumblers, in a milk bar Bob liked. It was a dark, cool place with big mirrors and tall stools with plastic leather tops, and old Formica on the counters.

Then south again, through a tiny town called Cambridge, which seemed to consist entirely of trees, and the sun rose higher and the tender blue of the early morning hardened into an unblemished enamel, and the distant purple line of high country grew closer.

Four miles out of a place called Tirau the road forked left to Rotorua, and the fat, gentle country was left behind us and we were on the volcanic plateau which is the heart of the North Island. There are three tall volcanoes there which have covered hundreds of square miles in layer after layer of ash and pumice, acid yellow, raw grey, and dead. The forests were burnt and burnt again, long before Man came, and the winters are bitter. The Maoris avoided it, invested it with gods and legends, and when the Europeans brought their farms and cattle, it defeated them; the winters mowed down the weakened animals, and bush sickness wasted them, and the scrub grew again where the empty farmsteads fell to pieces.

'So they said, well, we might as well plant a few trees,' said Bob. 'Pine trees took to it, you see. They didn't stint them-

selves, as you'll observe.' The road had plunged into the darkness of a pine forest, and as it rose to the crest of a long hill, I
could see the dark green sea of pines stretching out to the
horizon. 'A lot of this was planted in the depression,' said Bob.
'They reckoned if you were going to pay people to dig holes
and fill them in, you might as well put something in first. In
fact I believe they overdid it a bit. Too many of these trees
came up for felling at the same time: not enough sawmills.
Quite a lot are past their best.'

'Is this part of the country all pine trees?' I asked.

'Fair bit of it; but sometimes before the war they found out
what was killing the cows; the soil was short of a very small
amount of cobalt. Since then they've been top-dressing it on,
and breaking in the scrubland for farms all over the place. But
there's still a lot that's virtual desert; just scrub and fern. Army
uses it for manoeuvres. Bloody bleak in winter though; the cold
comes down off the mountains.'

We took a breather at the top of another of the hills, and I
could see the outlines of the volcanoes to the south, and to the
east the blue line of the axial ranges which are the boundary
of the plateau on that side. Hard up against them, I knew, lay
Hinaki, with whatever mystery it held, deep in its vastness of
pinus radiata. Overhead a top-dressing plane buzzed lazily
from north to south. We got back in the car.

Bob hadn't enquired very closely of my reasons for going to
Rotorua, and I think he sensed I didn't want to tell him. It was
slightly out of his route, but he decided to have lunch there
before pushing on south across the plateau towards the
Rangitiki.

The other thing about the plateau is tourism. Human beings
are attracted to violence of any sort, including geological
violence, and the plateau was well endowed. They came to
Rotorua in the nineteenth century to see the lava terraces and
boiling mud pools and steam vents and geysers, and to cure
their ailments in its sulphurous thermal pools. Today they also
have water-skiing on the lake, and the model Maori village with
model Maori guides in traditional Maori costume, and plastic

Maori gods in gift shops, and hotels designed and advertised in neon by people who admire Las Vegas.

There is a good fish restaurant by the lake, however, and I repaid Bob for the lift down by spending a little of Lord Hammersham's money on a thorough lunch. It got Bob talking about fishing, and that led him naturally to hunting and shooting, though not in the European sense. Both activities go together in New Zealand, and neither horses nor beaters are involved: just a rifle, a pack, a stout pair of boots and mile after mile of mountain bush. The target is deer. The excuse is that the deer destroy the bush. Bob was obviously an enthusiast for bush.

It set me thinking: two things. One, that I might need some of the equipment he was talking about, and two, that it would provide a very good excuse for heading where I was heading without going into long explanations. I asked him for a few details: and the lunch went on a little longer.

Then it was time for Bob to go, and we shook hands, and he got into the Holden. Before he pulled into the traffic he looked at me seriously and said, 'If you're ever needing . . . any assistance, mate, give us a ring. We're in the phone book. Don't hesitate, you know. And . . . er . . . look after yourself.' And he was gone.

I was on my own again. I spent the next hour on a concentrated spending spree, which is an activity at its most pleasurable when you have a good excuse and the money belongs to someone else. I went into the best sports shop in town and bought a blue Mountain Mule pack with a tubular aluminium frame, a down sleeping bag with a label saying Edmund Hillary had said it was okay, a 6 × 4 nylon tent with a groundsheet, a pair of 10 × 50 Zeiss binoculars, and a four-pound axe. 'It's to get at the dry wood inside trees,' said the man in the shop. 'Your tomahawk is lighter to carry, but when you need the weight to work with, it's useless. Take the four-pounder.'

I bought khaki cotton shorts and shirt and a pair of heavy-duty jeans, a pair of tramping boots (and supply of adhesive plaster and cotton wool) and an oilskin parka. Then I bought an aluminium billy, and went to a chemist's shop and got a selection of screw-top aluminium tubes which I filled with matches, tea, sugar, dried fruit and a variety of light and nutritious foods. Then I went to Bill Hamill's shop in Fenton Street and came away with a Parker Hale sporting conversion of a .303 S M L E, automatic action with telescopic sites, and a supply of ammunition. They're very careful about things like that in New Zealand. You have to get a piece of paper from the police before the sports shop will sell you a gun, and you have to take the gun back to the police when you've bought it so they can write down what it is exactly you've got. I did those things. I also sent a telegram to Hammersham. It might be the last he would get for his money.

Then it was time to go, and I checked by phone with the bus company about their service in my direction, and walked half a mile out of town in order to catch the bus when it came. They might not expect me to catch a bus, but they might have taken the precaution of watching the bus station.

When the bus came I went down to the back seat and took out my map and opened it and started thinking. It was a process I'd quite deliberately postponed at the moment I had opened the door of a room on the sixth floor of the Embassy Hotel, and met the eyes of the man with the toupee; I had shut down all speculative systems and concentrated on getting out in one piece and keeping my head down. Well, not entirely. The parts of my mind whose job it was to do these things had been silently chewing over the question of who the hell the man with the toupee had been, and how many friends he had. Whose side was he on, exactly? Not mine, anyway. Nobody in this game was on my side except a man in London who had taken out an insurance policy for me and given me a contract to sign. Was the toupee man one of the people behind the bugging and the Singapore attack? Somehow I didn't think so. That was the man in the tropical suit, I was sure, and the man in the tropical suit wasn't brooking any interference in the task of dealing with me. Anybody who was going to bother me, he

was going to kill. And then he was going to bother me himself.
When he found me. And then he was going to bother me good.

Back to the man in the toupee. The only thing I knew about
him was that he had just arrived in Auckland from an outdoor
trip near a place called Thames in the road from Auckland, a
map told me. I knew he'd been outdoors because of the mud
and the boots, and I guessed it was near Thames because the
only trophy I'd brought away from the sixth floor of the
Embassy Hotel, apart from my life, was a week-old copy of
the *Thames Courier*; and they didn't sell the *Thames Courier*
in Auckland newsagents, and when I read it I could see why.
What I couldn't see was why the man in the toupee was carrying it about with him. It had told him, and it now told me, that
somebody was running for mayor. Somebody was getting mar-
ried. Several people had died, and their relatives had written
small poems about it. The authorities were planning to mend
some holes in the roads. They'd got some new books for the
library. And a private citizen had thought he'd seen a meteorite
land in the hills behind the town. That was the only item that
could conceivably have some significance, and for the life of
me I couldn't conceive what that significance might be. Coromandel is a long way from Hinaki. Plant genetics are not, as
far as I know, greatly influenced by meteorites. And neither was
Jim Wells. And if the man in the toupee was a harmless old
meteorite hunter, why did he want to interview me and why
had the man in the tropical suit killed him? And how did he
know about me? Who had told him? Who was he working for?

I asked these questions but they didn't distract me from
recognizing the underlying fact, much as I didn't want to recognize it, or even come within speaking distance of it. The fact
was that I was being hunted not by one large, efficient, powerful, vicious organization, but by two.

I decided to concentrate on adding up the good points. There
were many.

The first one was that I was here at all. I had managed to
avoid one lot of surveillance and pick out who had been doing
the surveilling. I had managed to go to ground in the city and

get down to Rotorua without their picking me up again, I had reason to hope. I had got myself a cover and some protection and I was getting to within a few miles of Hinaki and all that remained was to reach it without them picking me up again first. Any of them.

It wouldn't be so easy this time; I didn't have the city to hide in. I looked through the windows of the bus, caked thick with dust and splashed with long streaks of mud. The forest lay on both sides of the road, and beneath the green the tree trunks stretched away into the darkness.

I looked at the map. It was an inch-to-the-mile Ordnance Survey job and eight years out of date. The forest was split into huge stands of timber, each roughly square, and the roads were part of the pattern. The access track to Hinaki led off the last minor road before the system petered out, and it would be a very simple matter indeed to keep an eye on anybody coming down that road, and to deal with him when he left it.

So I would have to keep off the roads, and when the bus dropped me, cut across through the timber. I would have to cross that minor road before getting into the Hinaki stand, but there was nothing I could do about that except cross it as far away from the access track as possible. Once over it would be simply a matter of getting through the forest to the research station itself without using the track. And a few other things.

The bus didn't have many scheduled stops along that highway, and the driver put me down where I asked him to. I waited till the bus was out of sight and then scrambled quickly up the yellow clay bank and climbed over the fence and entered the forest. I waited there for a moment, under the shadow of the trees, and listened for any sound other than the distant thump of timber-felling, but that was all. Beneath the trees the air was warm and still and slightly dusty and heavy with the scent of pine resin.

I set off across the block and the darkness beneath the branches deepened and the road receded into the distance. My feet slithered slightly on the smooth carpet of brown pine needles, but it was easy going. The lower branches had been pruned and I could walk fast and upright. I began to adjust to the weight of the pack. My boots felt fine.

It took me twenty minutes to cross the block, and when I was about a hundred yards from the edge I stopped and listened and then went on slowly and carefully. Ten yards away from the road I went flat on my stomach and began to wriggle over the pine needles to the fence. There was no sense in taking any chances.

The road was narrow, embedded about ten feet down clay banks on either side. The tarmac was new and clean and a thin layer of pine needles covered the edges.

It appeared to be empty. On the other side, the trees went on again. Hammersham's trees.

They appeared to be empty too.

I lay there for ten minutes, and nothing happened. I decided to give it another minute. I watched the second hand of my watch sweep steadily round to twelve and when it reached it I got up, stepped over the fence, and slithered down the bank. It took about two strides to get into the middle of the road, and when I had taken the second stride I heard the car coming.

It took one stride to cross the rest of the road, and when I was there I levered myself and my pack straight up the bank as though I was doing a chin-up. I got to my knees and then my feet in one movement and over the fence in another. Both movements were very brief. Then I flung myself forward and down on to a carpet of needles and lay there, breathing deep and listening.

The car came steadily down the road and about a hundred yards away it paused and changed gear and I thought it was going to stop and didn't know whether to run or stay; and then it drew alongside and the noise of the motor fitted over my head like a hood, and then it had passed me and it had not stopped and the noise of it died on the road till it was no more than the buzzing of an insect, and then it was gone. The silence descended again, and I began to get up. I had reached Hinaki and I was still operative. I breathed deep and adjusted the straps on the pack, and set off away from the road.

7   End of a Line

I set off on a course that was at a slight angle to that of the access track, so that I would draw steadily nearer the shallow valley in which it lay, but keep at a distance of between half and a quarter of a mile until I was almost at the research station. When I got there I'd think again.

Once more the light from the road died into the brown gloom of the trees and the scent of the pines rose like incense. The trees were planted in neat rows, and endless vistas of trunks stretched away in every direction until I began to feel I was in a box with mirrors on every wall. Except for the fact that I myself did not appear on any of the mirrors.

The air was warm, I sweated a little and the dust in the air settled on my face and stuck there.

I didn't feel a lot of apprehension because I didn't let myself do so. The pine forest seemed a neutral place, an antechamber, and all the nerve-endings which become so hyper-active when you sense danger, were quiet. Not sleeping, just taking a rest.

It was probably something to do with the carpet of pine needles. They softened every contour and cushioned every sound except that of my own breathing, which was loud because I wasn't used to walking with a 50lb pack on my back or carrying a rifle.

At thirty minutes I decided it was time to rest, and I slid down against a pine-trunk and stretched my legs and breathed in deeply.

I shouldn't have done that. The air didn't smell right. It carried the scent of something dead. It could have been a bird or a rat or something, but when I got up and walked a little way to avoid it, it persisted, and when I changed direction slightly – towards the road – it grew stronger. I weighed up the evidence. It was something large. I hadn't seen any large animals in the forest: as far as I knew there were none. I had better find out what it was.

I stopped again and squatted down and looked along each vista of trunks in turn. The floor of the forest rolled away towards the valley, smooth and unbroken except for a few thin branches . . . and one larger one. I walked towards it and the smell grew stronger, but it was strong all around there; and the pine needles around the branch lay just as smooth as those elsewhere. Except for one thing. They were darker. The rain leaches the colour from the needles lying on the surface until they are a pale tan. But those beneath stay brown longer, and someone had smoothed a heap of these needles over the surface. In the half-light the impression was of a huge, still pool of red liquid on the ground.

I went away then, to where the air was clearer, and filled my lungs with it. Then I went back to the log and began to scrape away at the needles, throwing them to one side in handfuls. I concentrated on the task of digging and kept my mind away from the question of what I was digging for.

A few inches down my knuckles touched something soft, and I scraped away some more, and then got up again to where the air was clearer, and breathed deep once more. Then I went back.

It had been a chest I had touched, and above the chest was a head, and the head belonged to Jim Wells. I could see that without looking at the photograph, and I could see why he was lying there too. Someone had shot him through the chest. Someone close to him. He had a shirt on that had once been white and now was black with blood.

His face didn't have a revealing expression on it. It was just dead. The next thing I noticed was that he had three hands.

I went away again, kept my stomach in control, breathed, and came back. I grasped him by the shoulders and pulled, and his head lolled back horribly, and then he was slumped over, lying on his side, and the third hand belonged to somebody else, and that somebody was lying beneath him, and he had been shot through the throat. I reached into my wallet and took out the photos of the three scientists at Hinaki and looked at them and looked at the face, and it was none of them. He had black hair and a beard. It hadn't been a memorable face even before it was dead. I walked far enough away to stop retching, calm down and start thinking.

The first thought that came into my head was: mission accomplished. Jim Wells found. No assistance necessary. No assistance possible.

Why, for God's sake? What the hell was so important about a damned tree that they had to kill the poor guy for? And whoever was with him. Who the hell was with him anyway?

I steeled myself and went back to the grave and looked again at the second occupant. Looking at his face again didn't tell me a thing. Lifting Jim Wells's arm away did. He had blue cotton under his fingernails. The other corpse had a blue cotton shirt on with a long rip in it.

I checked out some more things then, and they didn't tell me anything. I decided the time had come to get out of there and to get out of there fast. I should have walked towards the road. That would have been the sensible thing to do. Call in at a police station, cable Hammersham, and go home, fast. The sensible thing. Instead I started walking towards the research station. I was definitely insane.

While I walked I pulled the pieces apart and put them together and pulled them apart and put them together again and every time they didn't fit and all around the forest was as silent as that grave had been. I listened and it didn't tell me a thing.

Why had Jim Wells been in a fight – a fight to the death, it looked like – with an unknown bearded party? And if it had been a fight to the death, who had cleared up afterwards? And why? Why return Wells's hire car? I paused. That person had been an American. The man on the roof at Amalgamated House had been an American. Suddenly and involuntarily my mind selected an action replay of the encounter between Hammersham and the man on the roof, and I began to see how Jim Wells came to be under five inches of pine needles in a forest in New Zealand. I saw how members of the Central Intelligence Agency, if they had come across both bodies before they had been tidied away, might have been very interested to know who the middle-aged man with the blue cotton under his fingernails was. And who he worked for.

With a dead operative on their hands, they might even have done a little bugging.

I began to walk faster. The pieces might be starting to fit but I still couldn't see the picture. I could see the outlines of how Jim Wells came to be dead and how Hammersham came to have a man in a boiler suit on his roof. What I couldn't see was why.

That was the reason I was going to the research station. It was the only reason I could think of, anyway.

Another half-hour passed and with every hundred yards the atmosphere of the forest seemed to fill with another element. It wasn't one I could smell. But I could feel it. It was a menace. I kept going.

At last the ground began to slope steeply down to my right and I could see the access track through the trees. I stayed on the ridge. I couldn't see anyone or anything on the track.

Ten minutes later I saw the first building down through the trees, perhaps two hundred yards away. I dropped on to my stomach, wriggled the pack off, and took out the binoculars.

All the buildings were rectangular prefabs. At the bottom of the slope stood the shed where they kept the mechanical equipment and the Land-Rover and their small hydrostatic tractor. Next door there was a lavatory and next door to that a shed for the generator and at right angles to that the laboratory. At right angles to that stood the building they slept, ate and lived in. The fourth side of the small square clearing consisted of a greenhouse. Half the greenhouse was made of glass. Half of it was covered in some dark substance. Behind the greenhouse were four seed-beds. Beyond the seed-beds the forest started again.

There was no sign of life.

I made myself comfortable and went over every building with the binoculars and there was still no sign of life and no sign of anything being disturbed.

The super-tree stood a few yards from the greenhouse, above a cluster of seedlings about a quarter its size. It wasn't spectacularly big, but it looked somehow different from the other trees in the forest, and I knew it was the tree that had started all this. It stuck out.

Nobody seemed to have done anything to it. It just stood there.

I waited twenty minutes up on the ridge and then I took the rifle and loaded it and put the pack behind a tree and set off down the slope.

After a hundred yards I pulled in behind a tree and looked the compound over again. Still nothing. If they were waiting for me, they were waiting very patiently. Or they were dead.

I broke from the shadow of the trees and sprinted for the cover of the equipment shed and flung myself against it, panting. I stilled my breath and listened. Nothing. The wood was warm and smelt of creosote. I began to edge round to the door. It was a big door and when I pulled at it it wasn't locked and it creaked loudly as it opened. I propped it open with my foot and peered into the darkness inside.

Most of the shed was filled with a Land-Rover. I went in and let the door close behind me and edged along the gap between the Land-Rover and the wall. It was very dim now, because the only light came from one dirty window and it occurred to me how vulnerable I was, trapped between the machine and the wall. But nothing happened. I reached the front of the Land-Rover and it was a perfectly ordinary Land-Rover except for a bullet hole through the windscreen. I edged back again and opened the front door and there was a hole from the same bullet in the back of the driver's seat, a small tear in the fabric.

There was no blood. There were no bodies in the Land-Rover. The keys were still in the lock.

In front of the Land-Rover stood the hydrostatic tractor, and around it were chain saws, backpacks and tree-injection units, piles of rope and drums and so on. There were no more bullet holes, there was no blood, there were no bodies.

I knelt down on the floor. There was nothing underneath anything either.

I got out. When I closed the door behind me the sunlight dazzled me and I was blind for a moment until sight returned, with that odd effect of an old negative before the colour drains back into everything. I scanned the trees on the ridge, half expecting to see a silent figure there, waiting for me. There was no one.

There was nothing unexpected in the generating shed or the lavatory and I walked across the compound to the lab. It was locked. I went back to the shed and took the ladder I had seen hanging on the door and leant it against the wall and climbed up until I could see through the window.

The room was lined with shelves and the shelves were filled with files and papers and plant pots. There were three benches which filled most of the floor space and two were covered with a litter of Petri dishes, test tubes, retorts, microscopes and scientific instruments and some scales.

It wasn't orderly, but everything appeared to be undisturbed except for a fallen stool and a large retort, smashed on the floor. I looked thoughtfully at it through the window. If it had contained anything, it had gone and left no sign of its passing.

I came down off the ladder and went over to the greenhouse. It was hot in there, predictably, and it was full of seedlings. They didn't tell me anything, so I opened the door into the darkened part and looked inside. The infra-red bulbs hung from the ceiling, lifeless, because the generator wasn't going, and underneath them was the bare earth. No seedlings. Somebody had taken them away.

When I had done the greenhouse I walked over to the tree I had picked out from the ridge. I decided it was the tree I had thought it was. It looked almost the same as an ordinary pine, except that the needles were broader and more glade-like than usual and the branches less straight and regular. The bark was comparatively smooth and the trunk seemed to bulge and glow with good health. Nobody seemed to have disturbed it. It didn't look disturbed. It looked serene. The only outstanding feature was that it was four times as tall as the young trees around it.

So?

I turned to the last building, the living quarters, where logically I should have looked first, and which I had left till last for the same reason that I hadn't gone straight to the body of the man in the room on the sixth floor of the Embassy Hotel. I was chicken.

But don't dwell on it.

I looked up at the sun but it wasn't there. It had slipped behind the trees on the ridge top. The afternoon was waning. It would soon be dark. Get a move on.

The door was locked, so I took my ladder from the lab and tried the windows. There was nothing to be seen through them except silent furniture. No bodies.

The last window was not locked, and I opened it. It was a bedroom window. The bedroom appeared to be empty. I climbed in.

The bed was unmade and a thriller lay on the pillow. A pair of chest expanders hung from a peg on the wall. There was a pair of running-shoes under the bed. On the desk lay a bio-chemical text. I looked at the title and it didn't tell me anything, and I opened the door and stepped into the hallway.

It was empty. A door at the far end shut off the living-room and kitchen. I opened the door opposite me. It opened on to chaos.

The bedroom was the same size as the one I had just left, but it contained about five times the number of items and they were organized in a way which would have kept a team of searchers for any one item at it for weeks. It was incredible.

Books constituted a large proportion of the mess. They were piled everywhere and lay open or upside-down everywhere they weren't piled. There were racks of test tubes and Petri dishes. There were several dismembered electrical devices and the tools with which the deed had been done. Clothes and bed-clothes were wound around most things. There were two plates of sandwiches.

Of course somebody might have strip-searched the room, but I didn't think so. A mess like that takes time, patience and imagination to create. And there were still no bodies.

The third room was meticulously neat and the bed was made. Nearly all the clothes had gone from the hangers, except for some tramping clothes, a pair of tramping boots, and a pack. When I saw them something occurred to me. I went back into the other two rooms and checked. No boots. No packs.

And the sandwiches were very old.

There was a fourth room, but nobody slept there; it was used as a study and it didn't hold anything that interested me, and that left the kitchen and living-room.

I stood in front of the closed door for a moment, and then opened it very quickly, and if anybody had been sitting there waiting for me with a gun in his hand he could have picked me off before I had even made him out among the shadows. Because the room had filled with shadows, and evening was replacing afternoon and I had almost left it too late.

I went over the kitchen first. It contained nothing except dirty pans and dishes, and not much food, and then I went into the living-room and there was nothing in there except book-shelves, a table, two canvas chairs and a sofa. On the floor there was nothing except a couple of goatskins and a layer of dust. I know because I knelt down to have a look. It was that which saved me.

I was behind the sofa when I heard it, and I froze. It was a bump: the slight sound made as a forehead bumps against a pane of glass. Somebody was looking in the window.

Muscles I didn't know I had tightened all over my body like small hands.

There was a small scrabbling noise: the noise made by fingernails against a pane of glass. I felt very cold. And then I did a brave thing. Or maybe it was a stupid thing, but it was my bravery that impressed me at the time. I inched my head along the floor and peered up at the window.

Then I wished I hadn't done that. If I had been cold before, my guts were now packed in ice.

Because the face at the window was the face of the man in the toupee. And the man in the toupee was dead.

The face was distorted slightly, because it was pressed against the glass, but there was no mistaking those features and those tight black curls. The man in the toupee had come back from the dead.

I fought to control myself and managed it. Use your common sense, you idiot!

The man at the window was alive and corporeal, no doubt of that. But I had seen him in a hotel room hardly more than twenty-four hours before, dead. Who said so? I'd said so. Why? He was lying there. The man in the tropical suit had attacked him. His toupee had fallen off. Did you look at him close up? Did you check he wasn't just unconscious? Did you check he wasn't just shamming? No. No, I didn't do those things. You know why. Well, here he is now, come visiting. What are you going to do about it?

The face left the window, and I heard the door handle being turned. It was locked; I knew that much. And then he did the same thing as I had done. He set off round the building to see if any of the windows were open. And I knew, when he turned the corner, he would see the ladder. And he would use the ladder.

And then he would be in here with me.

I closed my eyes and let a small, strangled shriek make its way up my throat and die against the roof of my mouth. Then I got up silently, picked up the rifle from the sofa, took the safety catch off, and unlocked the front door. As I did so I heard the ladder shift slightly as the toupee man put his weight on it.

I opened the door and stepped out into the night and closed

the door very quietly behind me. The last sound I heard was the toupee man dropping from the window to the floor inside.

Bye, bye, Toop.

I walked briskly across the compound and up the ridge and into the trees. I walked along the ridge and found my pack and collapsed beside it and breathed properly for the first time since the face had appeared at the window.

Okay, Toop baby, what the hell are you doing here? What brings you to these parts, I'd like to know?

He was in there for twenty minutes and then the front door opened and a dark shape slipped out. He disappeared for a moment, and then a torch shone briefly across the clearing. It went off and I couldn't see anything and then it went on again. But not towards the access track. Not in the direction of the road. The other way. Into the forest. What the hell was he playing at?

I shouldered the pack and picked up the rifle and left the safety catch off and followed him.

He was about three hundred yards ahead of me and I kept it that way. He was putting the torch on every now and then when he came to some sort of obstacle, and it was easy enough to keep track of him. The ground began to slope upwards when the clearing ended and it continued to do so for perhaps a mile. The pine smell was even stronger at night. Then the torch stopped. So did I.

It flashed around in the same place for some time and after a while I sat down, watching it, cradling the rifle.

He was setting up camp. There was the red glow of a Primus in the blackness, and then the smell of frying bacon. Pause.

Quite a long pause. When it was over there was a new sound in the forest: the sound of static. I listened to the static for twenty minutes, and it was very boring. But at the end of the twenty minutes it was replaced by something much more interesting. Very faint, through the night, came a tiny bleeping noise. And after that there was a rustle of paper, and the torch came on, and I knew that Toop was studying a map. And then came the noises of someone preparing to get into his sleeping-bag, and I waited another hour, and moved away until there was a log between us, and I did the same thing. I slept quickly. I was exhausted.

It was dawn when I woke. The first sounds I heard on waking were the sounds of him leaving and before I was fully conscious I was jamming my boots on my feet, ramming the sleeping-bag in the pack, and plodding off after him.

It was easy at first because the trees were still in rows and he kept to one row and I kept to the one next door. But within the hour the slope in the ground grew steeper and less even and the regular rows petered out and the trees were unpruned, stunted and deformed, and it became a matter of dodging and peering. At six he sat down with his electrical equipment and after a while the bleeping came through the quiet air like a still small voice and he got up, altered direction slightly, and began to move faster. It was hard work.

Finally the ground began to climb with a real vengeance and we went with it and the pines gave up and we were on a ridge-top and in front of us was another world altogether.

The mountain ranges stretched away into the morning farther than it was possible to see, peak after peak, ridge after ridge, all of them solid with dark green bush. Tatters of mist hung about the tallest of them.

Hundreds of miles of mountains run the whole length of the North Island of New Zealand, great upthrusts of greywacke and jointed sandstone, torn into a sheer-sided maze of ridges and deep-etched valleys by the rains, every inch thick with native forest of beech and rimu, a great wall slicing off the eastern coastlands of the country from the rest. The Rimutukas, the Kawekas, the Kaimanawas, the Ureweras, lapped by the tamed pastureland foothills and plains, another world where men come on sufferance and do not stay. Toop gave them a swift, searching glance, spent several minutes with his map, and then set off up the ridge-top.

Before I followed him I turned to look below us, at the sea of pine trees flowing westwards over the immense plateau under a cobalt-blue sky, and, in the distance, at the three volcanoes at the centre of the island. From one of them a plume of smoke drifted slowly up into the sky. It was very quiet. As I turned and followed him into the shadow of the bush, the scent of the pines came to me for the last time, rising on the warming morning air.

It was very dark in the bush, much darker than it had been under the pines. The beeches and rimus towered a hundred feet and more thrusting their leaves towards the light. Parasites clung like slumbering snakes around their sheer trunks, and around their feet grew a tangle of ferns and creepers and smaller trees.

Everything dripped constantly, and where a shaft of sunlight lit up a leaf, little droplets of water sparkled like pieces of crystal. Beneath my feet the earth was rich with water, digesting a generation of dead matter to support the next generation of life. The air was full of moisture too, cool against the skin and motionless, as though it had never known a breeze. It didn't stop me sweating because the other characteristic of the ranges, apart from impenetrable bush, is slopes with a gradient of about one in two, and climbing slopes of one in two was not something I was physically ready for. Cities do that to you. My calves jittered in anguish and then exploded into a series of cramps. The straps of my pack bit through the foam pads and into the flesh of my shoulders; air rasped in and out of my lungs like sandpaper and every inch of my body ached.

That was the easy part. After a while we gave up climbing and started crawling, hauling ourselves up the ridgeback on roots and creepers while the rich humus spread steadily over our clothes. My body began to crave rest the way a stomach craves food. Every time I caught a glimpse of Toop's bush shirt through the foliage up ahead, I hated him, and when I wasn't hating him I was pitying myself.

Our ridge was a tributary ridge, twisting its way up to the line of a larger one, and it took us most of the morning to get to its end, and when we came to a break in the trees and could see where we were, the sight was not a heartening one. Ahead of us lay a formless, jagged heap of ranges, monotonously green, endlessly twisted, and deadly. Each of those slopes would demand effort like we had made this morning and effort like that can make mincemeat of you if you're not ready for it. I wasn't ready for it.

Toop collapsed about two hundred yards ahead, leant against a tree trunk and took out the little grey box which gave out the bleeps. When he'd tuned to its music he looked at his map and worked on his compass for a while. Then he ate. I ate. Then we set off. It felt no better than the morning. In fact it felt worse.

We headed south along the ridgeback for forty minutes, and at the end of that time he set off to the left, off the ridge and down, and it was almost as steep as it had been coming up and all the muscles that had not been exercised in the climb were jolted into action by the descent. I had the harder job. I had to come down fast enough to keep up and not so fast as to join up. I was still sweating. When we reached the bottom of the valley, in front of us, running silent beneath the trees, lay the first river. Toop looked at it for a moment, filled his water bottle and waded straight across, thigh deep. I waited briefly and followed him, my boots slithering on the slimed rocks of the bed, and then I was on the other side and the water was cascading off me and I was under the trees again and it was uphill work.

All afternoon we hacked our way diagonally across the valley-face, still south, and with every hour that passed the darkness and silence of the bush began to oppress me more and I could not prevent myself from thinking about what would happen if I lost Toop. What would happen, I knew, would be that I would become lost, because it was that sort of country, and when I became lost, it would only be a matter of time.

And if I did not lose Toop, but he found me instead, it would be a matter of even less time. And I had no one to blame for it except myself. The climb went on.

Gradually the character of the forest began to change, and the rimus disappeared and there was nothing but beech trees, and as the afternoon waned patches of moss and lichen began to appear on the trunks and with each half-mile the trees were smaller and stunted and the moss and lichen grew larger; and then the mist came.

It came on very suddenly, thick, grey and opaque, and sounds came through it unnaturally loud, and beneath our boots the earth squelched and sucked like an old man eating, and the dark shapes of the dwarfed trees shifted in the mist like uneasy spectators. Small pearls of moisture clung to the fibres of my jersey. I went on climbing. The mist thickened.

Then I felt around me that the landscape had changed, and we had come up on to the ridge-top, and all around us the ground fell away into valleys such as that from which we had climbed.

And I knew I had lost Toop.

I stopped. I listened. I could hear twigs breaking yards away and tiny furtive rustlings in the undergrowth. Where the hell was he?

I walked forward four paces and a twisted shape loomed up ahead. I walked straight past it and stopped again. There was a cough to the right. Something like a cough. I plunged off to the right and there was nothing. And then it occurred to me. Somewhere out there Toop was levelling his pistol at me, just waiting till I got close enough. He'd known I'd been following him. He'd known all along. He'd just been waiting for the right moment. And this was it.

I fought that one down and took another direction, following a slight sound, and again there was nothing, and another direction, and I was wrong again. I cursed the mist under my breath and began to stumble downward off the ridge to get out of it, and the earth sucked and chuckled grimly beneath my boots; the dead and rotten branches detonated as I stepped on them and tatters of delicate cobwebs trailed from my legs like little flags of defeat.

And then the mist began to thin and I could see five, ten, twenty feet ahead and the trees were real trees and I was down out of the mist. But I had lost Toop. I was quite alone.

I stood there on the edge of the cloud for perhaps fifteen

minutes, waiting, watching to see if a shape came down from the mountain-top, but there was nothing.

I started to descend through the trees, my stomach filled with a sick mixture of fear and failure, and when the slope split into two ridges I took the right-hand one without thinking and just kept going. The forest thickened again and the green world closed around me once more, and deep in the shallow valley to my left I could see a stream snaking around the roots of the trees, and it was a bright, cheerful stream so I let my eye follow it unthinkingly.

And it was then that I saw the satellite.

9 Focus

It was like a blow in the face. I came to a dead halt, staring at the broken, burnt trees and the silver spheroid head among the charred wood and smashed greenery. It was as though somebody had twisted the lens on a camera and everything – almost everything – had come into focus.

There were two bulges, on either side of the spheroid shape, and it looked like a giant insect peering up out of its nest.

It was a Russian satellite, that much I knew because of the shape. Beneath the sphere was a tapering cylinder with the remains of a ring of canisters around it and below that, smashed into the ground, a mass of crushed pipes. The machine stood drunkenly to attention in its little circle of devastation, the silver streaked with carbon from the fires that had raged all about. A fallen branch lay across it like an arm trying to push it back into the ground.

I went forward involuntarily to run my hand over the beautifully engineered surface, and as I did so I began to spool the film of what had happened through my mind to see what it looked like now I had crashed here in the mountains before the movie started.

I had just got past the opening credits when the gun cracked behind me. The bullet hit metal and richocheted off into the bush, whining evilly. I threw myself face downwards in the mud and the next shot smashed me into the earth, tearing through the broad blue target of my pack and ending its career in the binoculars. I launched myself forward along the ground until the satellite was between me and Toop while the next shot thudded into a branch inches from my fingers. I levered myself upright and tore at the rifle and fumbled the safety catch off while part of my head said: So you lost him, did you, baby? All alone, huh? What did you think that bleeping was? The top ten . . . ? And then I had the rifle up at my shoulder and aimed at where the shots had come from and I squeezed the trigger and the noise hit me as though someone had swung at my ear with a bell, and the recoil slammed painfully into my shoulder. I let go of the trigger then, because I remembered that automatics hog ammunition and if I ran out of ammunition I wasn't going to get time to reload. There was a movement in the undergrowth and I loosed off again and the part of my mind that made comments like that noted that I was much calmer than I had any right to be, which was because my imagination hadn't started working yet, and then the other part said Down! and I did it as the next shots ploughed into the earth beside me.

There was a flash of colour in the undergrowth and I fired again and there was a scream and then there was no more movement and I knew I had hit him.

The sound reverberated around the valley and died. The acrid smell of cordite floated away into the air and there was nothing but silence. I stared at the patch of green where I had seen the shirt until my eyes began to go out of focus and there was no more movement and no more noise and I thought: Is he dead?

Toop had done this to me before and I could see him, in my mind, lying there with his gun ready to take me when I came looking for him. I will be patient, I said, I will sit here until he tires of his game or until I am sure he is dead, because he is a professional and I am an amateur and I could not afford to let the difference tell again. I took the pack off and waited. I waited what must have been fifteen minutes, and not once did I let that patch of bush out of my sight. When fifteen minutes had passed I shifted position, and the second that I did so he fired from behind me, from the other side of the valley. The first shot hit the rifle and tore it from my hands and then I was running as if I had never run before for the cover of the trees, and the bullets thudded into the ground behind me like punctuation marks.

Now I was out of the charred circle and there was thick undergrowth in front of me and I threw myself into it as though it was a pool and began to crawl furiously up the valley slope. The firing didn't stop. It was wet down there and the light was entirely green. The tree trunks up ahead looked like tower blocks. Wet earth plastered itself on to my face.

Then the bullets stopped and so did I. There was a rotten log draped with vegetation and I wriggled behind it and lay there, listening. There was a sudden crashing somewhere across the valley and then silence. Far above my head a droplet of water detached itself from a leaf and plunged down through the still air, exploding on the surface of the log; a tiny cataclysm. A small black beetle which I did not recognize walked in huge, purposeful zigzags along a fern frond. I still couldn't hear anything. I drew in my feet and made myself as small as possible.

When the noise came it was some way off, but down on the floor of the forest it sounded very loud and very close, and I had to steady myself and tell myself how far away it was. It got closer, and in the stillness the ceaseless crashing and breaking of roots and stems was like the roar of an oncoming tidal wave. I told myself to keep still, to let it pass, but I felt the way a coiled spring feels when you compress it in your hand.

He kept on coming. He chose the right path, and suddenly a rotten branch squelched twelve inches away, on the other side of the log, and a bird flew up, screaming. It was the first forest bird I'd come across yet and why the goddam thing had to wait until Toop arrived before taking fright I don't know, but that was very nearly it. The noise set off reflexes in Toop and he didn't pause to restrain them. He pulled the trigger and loosed off, and the hands around the spring were released and I launched myself from behind the log in a way that must have terrified him. I went straight up the slope and the bullets began to follow me but not fast enough; and then my foot caught in

a root and I cannoned into the ground at about the same speed
I had leapt up from behind the log. Head first.

I whirled round again before the concussion had time to sink
in and Toop was a yard away, his rifle aimed straight at me.
He was reloading.

I went straight at him and hit him hard in the chest with both
arms and he went over backwards down the slope. As he went
he took hold of the rifle barrel with his free hand and swung
it at me like a club. It took me on the side of the head and this
time things really did go black, very briefly.

And then a voice said: 'Okay, that's enough. Stop!' And a
man came down the valley-side with a rifle in his hands.

10 Wide Angle Lens

He was built like an ox, and on top of his squarish head was a thatch of thick, curly, fair hair. The black oilskin parka he wore looked as if it was wrapped around a big rock. He was thirty-two years old and his name was Fielding. Sam Fielding. Bill Hawk had lured him away from the Department of Scientific and Industrial Research, up to Hinaki to work on the tree with him. He was, the dossier said, highly intelligent.

And he held a rifle with a very steady hand.

'Would you place that rifle on the ground, mate, before it goes off,' he said to Toop. Toop turned and looked at him. I could see him calculating whether he could swing the gun round, aim and fire before Fielding brought him down, and deciding that he couldn't, he acted swiftly on the decision.

'My name is Karyanin, Joseph Karyanin, a businessman and a visitor to your country. I have been viciously attacked. I am grateful that you have come to my aid in time.' He spoke crisply and convincingly, with a thick Middle-European accent. He was good. His eyes flashed with a righteous indignation and his voice trembled with it. If he hadn't been about to kill me fifteen seconds before I'd have believed him.

Fielding looked steadily at him and said: 'Put the gun down, mate, immediately.' Karyanin stood still for a moment and then put the rifle at his feet. 'Kick it away,' said Fielding. He kicked it away.

'I protest,' Karyanin said. 'I am a tourist in your country, a hunter, and I have been attacked by this hooligan. You saw me merely defending myself. If you take any action against me I will report you to the authorities.'

Fielding turned to me. 'And you, mate?'

I said, 'I'd like to give you a document. May I reach into my jacket?'

'Slowly.'

I took out the credentials Hammersham had given me to hand to Jim Wells. Jim wasn't going to want to see them any more. I gave them to Fielding. He read them through and breathed deeply. Then he said, jerking his head at Karyanin, 'Who's this then?'

'No tourist, I'll tell you that much. He's been looking for what's in the valley there for some days, with a radio receiver. I've been following him since Hinaki. I'd say he's from the owners.'

Fielding walked closer to Karyanin. 'Care to do a bit of explaining, my friend?' Karyanin just looked at him, his red lips compressed into a thin line. Suddenly Fielding's fist shot out and hit him just below the ear. He gave a grunt and collapsed. There was something very shocking about that act; its suddenness, I think, rather than its brutality. Fielding had the build of a fighter, but he also seemed very stolid, almost wooden. It was unnerving to see him move so fast.

He knelt beside Karyanin and began methodically going through his pockets. He called over his shoulder to me. 'Up the bank fifty yards is my pack. There's rope in there and a knife. Bring it, would you?'

I did as he said and handed them over. I had an unpleasant vision of him thrusting the knife between the Russian's ribs, but he simply finished his search, took the rope, trussed Karyanin thoroughly with it and stuck the knife into the rotten log a few feet away. Then he stood up.

'I assume he has a pack and provisions about the place somewhere?'

'He had a while back. Why, do you want to search them?'

'Waste of time. Everything in his pockets was neutral, nothing much to go on, and I think the same will apply to his gear. No, I just don't want the bastard to die of exposure. He'll come round in a minute and he should be able to cut himself loose after a while. We'll just act on the assumption that he's a Russian until we get information to the contrary: there's no time to waste trying to confirm it. We'd better get a move on. We don't want him following us. Where's your gear?'

We went back to the satellite and picked up the torn pack and the rifle. Fielding looked the satellite over briefly and swore at it. 'Bloody thing,' he said. I looked at him speculatively. 'Explanations later,' he said shortly. 'We've got a way to go and the quicker we do it the better. Come on.'

The valley twisted round sharply after less than a quarter of a mile, and we climbed out of it, up a ridge heavy with bush. When we got to the top of the ridge, I was panting and the light had begun to fade. Fielding didn't pause. He seemed to be deep in thought, too preoccupied with whatever was going on to take any real notice of me. We tramped in silence along the ridge-back while the forest faded into blackness around us. After twenty minutes we set off down a spur and the bush thinned. There was a track of sorts. We were going down steeply and the narrow walls of a valley rose above us as we descended.

Quite abruptly we were out of the trees and in a clearing. At the far end of the clearing, near the head of the valley, stood a rough hut made of corrugated iron. It had a chimney built with river stones, and smoke drifted from it into the darkness. It had a single window, yellow with the light from a hurricane lamp. It looked full of welcome after the night-tramp. But about the valley itself there was an unnatural stillness, as if it was waiting for something.

It was.

We crossed a small stream that was making a lot of noise in the way that streams seem to do at night, and walked up to the hut across a bare patch of ground covered with half-chopped logs and branches.

'Well,' said Fielding. 'This is home.'

The interior of the hut was impressive. It was furnished with four wooden bunks and a table that looked as if it had been made with an adze. Around the table were four thick slices of tree. They were the chairs.

The corrugated iron walls were solidly plastered, like a Victorian screen, with a montage of pin-ups dating from a period when pin-ups were a lot more modest than they are now, augmented by scenic pictures of New Zealand and advertisements for goods long-forgotten visitors had wished to contemplate. These were mainly tractors and various brands of beer. Any space not covered by pictures was stuck with old newspapers to keep out the draughts.

The hut would have looked like just another of the temporary shelters for trampers that are dotted about the New Zealand bush, if it had not been for the incredible tangle of equipment, food and clothing that filled it. The mess bore the stamp of the man whose room I had visited at Hinaki. And he was here now, in front of the fire, seated on one of the tree stumps, holding a toasting fork made out of fencing wire. His name was Bill Hawk.

Bill Hawk was a big man too, but not like Sam Fielding. He was shaped like a huge bear with a big, contented, sleepy face that reminded me irresistibly of an owl. He wore cheap National Health glasses with thick lenses and he smoked a pipe; behind the glasses his eyes peered out shrewdly. Sam introduced me and showed him Hammersham's letter. Hawk held it close to his face and studied it for a moment. Then he looked at me.

'Sit down, my boy, sit down.' He waved vaguely at the debris with the toasting fork. I moved a plate, a condenser and a box of ammunition from one of the logs and sat down.

'I suppose you want to know how Jim Wells came to die?' he said.

'Right. I found the bodies.'

'And surmised?'

I looked at them both. Bill was regarding me intently. Sam was concentrating on pouring out three mugs of tea. And I mean concentrating.

'Wells had half the other guy's shirt under his fingernails,' I said. 'But having your shirt torn isn't usually fatal. And Jim Wells wasn't exactly Wild Bill Hickok.'

Neither of them said anything. Sam finished pouring the tea and handed out the mugs. Bill Hawk said: 'Right, absolutely right. But look, it'll make things easier if we know what you know. Give us a brief resumé.'

And I did.

'I can understand why you're mystified,' said Bill Hawk when I had finished. 'I'm not sure I can explain it all, but I'll try. It starts, as you may imagine, with the space capsule.' He paused, as though reluctant to start.

'The last information I have is when you sent your report on the tree to London,' I said helpfully. 'You'd had some success. How does that fit in?'

'Ah, yes. It seems a long time ago. In fact it seems a very small affair, compared with this. Did you see the tree at Hinaki, by any chance?'

'Yes, I did. It looked very healthy.'

'Good, good. Yes . . .' And he paused again for a moment. 'Well, shortly after we sent that report Lord Hammersham cabled that Wells would be coming to have a look at our work. He gave us a date and we decided it gave us time to give ourselves a holiday and do some tramping up here in the mountains. At least that was Sam's idea. Our colleague, Robertson, has been on leave for the last month on family business, not due back for some time. I felt like a break, so Sam and I set off.

'We spent an energetic few days gallivanting about, collecting a few specimens, that sort of thing, using this place as a base. On our last night we were about to descend into the valley after a long day out, when Sam saw what appeared to be a meteorite. We watched it come down and it looked as though it wasn't far away. Next morning we set out to see whether we could find it.'

'And you did find it,' I said.

'We did,' said Bill. 'A Russian satellite, one of the Cosmos series. Clearly it had not been programmed to come down where it did; you've seen how it was damaged in re-entry and landing.' He looked slightly embarrassed. 'The damage was

sufficient to render it accessible to those with a little knowledge of these things.'

I could imagine the scene: the two of them, standing on the
edge of that hidden valley. Neither of them would have been
able to resist the temptation.

'What was in it?' I said.

Bill looked up at me. 'It contained a small biological war-
fare laboratory,' he said quietly. There was silence for a time.
Sam said, 'We thought at first it was some sort of bomb – a
biological bomb.'

'Then we revised that,' said Bill. 'There didn't appear to be
any trigger mechanism, for one thing. It seemed to be part of
the development process for just such a device. I think that
they were experimenting to find out what effects long periods
in space have on pathogens of the sort they were intending to
use.'

'You mean whether the radiation would cause mutations,
that sort of thing?'

'Exactly. And in fact it had. One of the creatures they sent
up there had come down in a distinctly different form, I believe,
from the form in which it went up.

'We took the contents back to Hinaki under the strictest conditions and killed each unpleasant specimen one by one, except
one: the mutation. Because the creature which had mutated
was not a disease-causing organism at all. It was in fact a
fungus.' He picked up the condenser and squeezed it hard between thumb and forefinger. 'What part they had intended it to
play in their unpleasant games I do not know. But what I did
realize was this: the fungus in question may be one of the most
important creatures ever to enter the history of the human
race.' He stopped and looked hard into the fire for a few
moments. I looked in there too and then opened my mouth to
ask him what he meant by it. Sam said, 'We're getting ahead
of ourselves. You want all your questions answered. Well, we
were back in the lab on the day that Wells was due to arrive,
doing our analysis. I'll spare you the scientific details, but it

was complex and time-consuming. We were pretty absorbed. Right in the middle of it there was a knock on the door. We put down what we were doing and opened it, thinking Wells had arrived early. We were wrong. It was an American, a youngish guy, with a black beard, a good yarn, and when that was no use to him, a gun. We obviously weren't the only ones to have seen the satellite come down. We were probably the only ones to have seen it with the naked eye, but that's not the only way. The Americans have got tracking stations all over the world. They probably spotted it straight away when the orbit altered some time before it actually came down. When it looked as though it was about to re-enter, they would have pulled out all the stops to try to get hold of it.'

'Do you mean they already knew that it had some sort of military significance?' I asked.

'Probably not,' Sam said. 'Some of the Cosmos series are quite straightforward scientific satellites; some of them are military. As a rule of course they just don't get to see them. There's quite enough Russian territory for the Soviets to be able to organize planned re-entries discreetly. It was only a malfunction that brought this one down somewhere the Americans had a chance of getting hold of it. They would have been very curious indeed. And extremely eager.'

'Would the New Zealand Government have been involved?'

'The odds are against it,' Sam replied. 'They don't maintain an extensive system of tracking stations themselves, and the Americans probably wouldn't have asked for their help. Under international law the satellite would have had to be returned to the owners. A small country like New Zealand tends to stick to the letter of international law. Of course the Russians would have been wild to get the thing back themselves: they didn't want anyone knowing what they had been up to – there were too many broken treaties in that capsule. But they couldn't ask the New Zealanders for help either, considering the fact that what they were asking them to give back was a load of bugs vicious enough to wipe out the entire country. So both sides have had to operate very secretly indeed.

'Our secret agent claimed he was a forestry worker looking for a base about fifteen miles away from us. He stood there at the door, telling us how he came to be lost and raking a very beady eye over everything on the work bench. There was nothing we could do to stop him. If he knew the sort of things he was looking for it would have been obvious to him that we'd already found it: there were too many ampoules with Cyrillic script engraved on them. He thanked us for our help, turned to go, and spun round with a gun in his hand, marched us over to the generator shed and locked us in. The slimy bastard. It didn't take me long to smash the door down but we were just too late. He'd cleared out the lab and hijacked the Land-Rover. He'd thought that would scupper us, but it didn't. You may have noticed a little hydrostatic tractor in the shed. It's not fast but it is designed for that sort of country. It meant we didn't have to stick to the track. We started her up, shot straight out of the shed and into the trees; once there we could cut across a big loop in the track, and we nearly got there in time. Very bloody nearly.'

'He got away?'

'No,' said Sam. 'There'd have been more activity round here where poor Jim Wells came in. Literally came in – drove right up the track at the same time as the American was driving down it: they met half-way. They stopped about three feet from each other. There was no way around.'

He stopped talking and contemplated me long and thoughtfully. Then he came to a decision.

'Jim got out. The C I A got out, gun in hand, naturally. I put my foot down and went straight at them, down the slope. Great move: C I A spins round and starts firing. Jim goes for the gun, tries to stop him, and the next minute the poor sod's lying on his back covered in blood. I don't remember stopping the tractor: I don't remember jumping; I just remember my shoulder sinking into that guy's guts before we went down. I never touched the gun, never laid a hand on it; he pulled the trigger himself. Bloody deafened me, couldn't hear a thing for hours: but it killed him. Right through the throat. He was dead within a minute. I reckon Jim must have died instantly.'

He poured the rest of his tea down his throat in one long swallow. 'So there we were with two corpses on our hands and enough blood to have a bath in. Perhaps you can see why we didn't go to the police.'

'Yeah,' I said. 'I can see.' And I could. 'What did you do?' I asked at last, if only to break the silence.

'Well,' said Bill, 'that was a facer at the time. It may be that we made the wrong decision, I don't know. We were both in a state of shock, as you may imagine. We decided to finish what we had to finish. We decided our overriding responsibility was to find out for certain if what had come out of the Cosmos was what we thought it was. We went back to Hinaki, removed all traces of our having been there recently, and headed out into the bush. There was nothing obviously suggesting that either of us were connected in any way with what had happened. Rightly or wrongly, we decided to leave it like that.'

'So when the C I A came along to find out what had happened to their man,' I said, 'they naturally jumped to the conclusion that his death was the result of enemy action. No wonder they tried to find out who did it. And when they got back to Hammersham and found out I was going out after Jim Wells I suppose it's also hardly surprising they bothered me the way they did.' Then a thought struck me.

'But they can't have known that their bloke had actually hit the jackpot – that he'd actually found where the satellite came down, can they?'

'No,' said Sam. 'There'd have been more activity round here if they had; they must have been bloody suspicious, but we didn't leave any evidence, and they had a hell of a lot of other possibilities to check out as well, don't forget. If I'd been in their shoes I'd have been chasing the Russians round. After all, the Russians had to have a homing device. The odds were on them getting to the Cosmos first.'

'And the Russians were searching the Coromandel Peninsula,' I said. 'I told you about that souvenir I got from the Embassy Hotel. Have a look.' And I fished out of my shirt pocket the folded pad of local newspaper that I'd taken from Karyanin's body. It made sense now. I handed it to Bill. 'See that item on the meteorite? Karyanin had just come from there when I came across him in Auckland. It looks as though you had a bit of luck. A Natural Phenomenon drew their fire.'

'Right,' said Bill. 'I'm not surprised. What one doesn't realize is the amount of tail chasing in this game. Not only has each side got to put every effort into reaching *its* goal, but it's also got to know what the other side is doing. The Americans find out the Russians are searching the Coromandel. They follow. The Russians find out that the Americans are searching for the owner of Hinaki: they come here. It can't be long before the C I A comes back here to check out what the Russians are up to. It's a very trying business.'

There was a pause. I cogitated. There was one highly significant point on which I had not been enlightened. What the hell had these two found in that spacecraft that was so vitally significant to the human race?

I asked them.

I didn't get an answer. Not then, not there. There was too much noise. The noise, that is, of the Astazou I I I B engine of a Westland Gazelle Helicopter with a speed of 192 mph, a range of 200 miles and bodywork in red and white, hovering a foot above the roof of a corrugated iron hut.

The guests had arrived.

11   The Man with the Passenger

The Westland must have had a landing spotlight, and the pilot must have been good because he barely used it. Even before the motors died the spot was swivelled so that a powerful white beam shot through the window of the hut and dazzled us. They must have virtually leapt from the machine as it came down too because it seemed that at the same moment that the light hit us, the door burst open and the room was filled with men.

But none of them carried guns. Three of them wore spectacles. One of them carried a briefcase. They all wore suits. And around the left sleeve of each of their jackets was an armband. It read: World Health Organization.

'Gentlemen, I am truly sorry to intrude like this,' said the oldest of them, stepping forward. He was a tall, thin man with a thick shock of grey hair and horn-rimmed spectacles. He was an American. 'My name is Dr Bede, Dr Oliver Bede of the World Health Organization. My colleagues and I are on a very urgent mission and we seek your help. You have been hunting in this area – is that correct?' Nobody contradicted him. 'Then we would like to know if any of you have seen either a meteorite or shooting star or something resembling that come down here during the last week?' Still nobody said anything, so he went on: 'The reason I ask is not because we are looking for a meteorite. We are looking for a space capsule, a satellite, which has crash-landed in this area very recently.'

'What exactly has the World Health Organization got to do with satellites?' said Sam. 'And would you mind turning that damn light off – I can't see.'

'Certainly, gentlemen, my apologies,' said Bede, and one of the men with him shouted something to whoever was outside in the Gazelle and the light died. The others began to sit down and plant themselves around the room. There were four of them altogether. We shifted on our seats to face them.

'I must ask for your assurance that what I have to say will be treated in confidence,' said Bede, his briefcase on his knees. He leant forward earnestly and I noticed, irrelevantly, that his fingernails were very neatly trimmed. 'For the simple reason that it could cause a lot of unnecessary panic if it became public. The satellite we are searching for was sent into orbit by the Soviet Union, with the object of making certain biological experiments with micro-organisms – in the interests, needless to say, of world health. There was a malfunction in the vehicle and we believe it has landed somewhere in this area of New Zealand. That much the tracking stations have been able to establish. The involvement of the World Health Organization stems from the fact that some of the micro-organisms concerned are pathogens – that is to say, disease-causing. If they escaped they could cause widespread loss of life. It is therefore absolutely imperative that we find it and take precautions. If you can help us in any way, we would be most grateful.' His eyes sought to meet each of ours in turn. He steepled his neat fingers, the way doctors do. There was a light sheen of sweat on his brow.

The question was, who was he? And whoever he was, what the hell were we going to do about it? I looked at Sam and Bill. They were thinking the same thing.

'I think we might be able to help you,' said Sam. 'About a week ago we saw what looked like a meteorite coming down about three or four miles from here. When you go outside, you should be able to see a peak to the north-west silhouetted against the ridge-top. It came down somewhere near there. To be quite honest, we went to have a look for the thing, but had no luck. But we're sure something came down in that area, eh?' and he turned to Bill and me. Bill seemed to want to say something more, but Sam's expression stopped him.

'Gentlemen, this is good news,' said Bede, standing up excitedly. 'It may well be what we are looking for.' He turned to face his men. 'Look, in view of the urgency of this matter, would one of you be kind enough to accompany us in the helicopter to the approximate area you think the vehicle landed?'

'It'll be too dark to do anything tonight,' said Sam. 'If it has gone down it will be in dense bush. You haven't a hope of spotting it in the dark.'

'Oh, by no means, young man,' said Bede, smiling. 'You've seen our spotlight. We have infra-red equipment too, and a receiver which could pick up any signals, however weak, the satellite is sending out – provided we are close enough. If we could just establish where this thing is, we could set in motion the operation necessary to recover it. And frankly, my friends, the situation is so urgent and we have wasted so much time in false trails already that there is no time to lose. I know none of you will want to leave your fireside at this time of night, but, well, human lives are at stake. Would *one* of you come?'

It was a powerful appeal. I glanced at Bill and Sam and I could see what they were weighing up. If this was a W H O team and we sent them on their way we could be passing up the one opportunity we had to set things right.

If it was not, and we refused to help, it would look very odd indeed.

I rose. 'I'll come with you,' I said.

Bill and Sam looked up at me, startled, and then I saw understanding in Sam's eyes. There was nothing to lose by this gambit. I didn't have whatever they had taken from the capsule – they did. By getting the W H O people out of their hair for a while I would give them the elbow-room they needed. And by going with Bede and his boys I would have the chance to decide if they were who they said they were. If they weren't, of course, I might not come back.

Dr Bede stepped up to me and took me by the hand and pumped it hard. 'I am most grateful, sir, I really am. We will be as brief as possible. Now – ' and he turned to Bill and Sam – 'there isn't a lot of room in the helicopter and if your friend here is coming with us, I wonder if two of my colleagues –

Dr Baker here and Dr Elliott – could remain with you until we return. No problem? Very good. Then let's be going.'

It was neatly done. As he said those words I had a sudden and sickening fear that I was wrong; that these men were no more from the World Health Organization than I was. And that they had us exactly where they wanted us. They had a hostage and Bill and Sam had two guards.

And they were taking me up in the helicopter.

I told myself to shut up and stop being so goddam nervous. If ever there was a kindly old physician out on a mission of mercy it was Dr Oliver Bede. I followed him out of the door. One of his colleagues came out behind me. He was a big man. I couldn't decide whether he looked like a doctor or not.

The Westland was parked in the middle of the clearing beside the little stream. It was a big machine, one of those helicopters that seem to consist entirely of a large Perspex bubble. As we came out the pilot turned the engine on again and the rotors began to turn slowly.

We stopped half-way across and Bede turned to me and said: 'Which is the peak your friend said you could identify?'

I had, of course, no idea.

'You'll have to wait a moment,' I said. 'My eyes aren't accustomed to the dark yet.'

'Never mind, never mind,' said Bede. 'We'll set off in a north-westerly direction and I'm sure it will become quite clear. Now, if you'll just follow me. Mind the steps,' and he clambered into the helicopter ahead of me and said a few words to the pilot. I put my foot on the first step and pulled myself upwards. Then I stopped suddenly, half-way up. I had seen the pilot's face.

He wore headphones, and a baseball cap with a big peak. The collar of his jacket was turned up against the cold. But that didn't stop me from recognizing him.

It was the man in the tropical suit. The man who had slugged Karyanin. The man who had been hunting me in the Embassy Hotel.

His eyes still gleamed with the same weird predatory light; and fear still sat on his shoulder like a passenger. The same magnetic force which had so nearly drawn me to him in Auckland hit me now, and I felt certain that he knew me and could see right through me.

I had to fight to hold down the panic. He didn't know me. He hadn't seen me and I had seen him. Keep cool.

'This is Mr Murdoch, who is acting as our pilot,' said Bede, grasping my arm and hauling me up. Even as he did so some trick of the light from the instrument panel caught his forehead. The thatch of grey hair was a wig.

'Sit down, sit down,' he said. 'Here, let me strap you in.' And he leant over and buckled my seat belt. Then the other man climbed in after me and shut the door. I glanced at the way he did it, casually and with desperate concentration. When he sat down the tiny cockpit was full. Very full.

'North-west,' said Bede to Murdoch. 'We head north-west, don't we?'

I had to fight to give a grunt of assent. All I could think about were the stories from Vietnam about G Is dropping people out of helicopters for kicks. I caught Murdoch's glance. He was the sort of person who would enjoy that. 'There's some peak, huh?' he said. His voice sounded like water disappearing down a plug-hole. As he spoke he moved the throttle and the chopper began to rise. I felt as though I was trapped inside a tin can with a gang of scorpions. The scream of the engines and the noise of the rotors seemed to crose over me, like water when you're sinking. Suddenly fear, panic and claustrophobia peaked together, and I acted.

I leant over towards Murdoch and unbuckled the seat belt with one hand as I did so, hiding the movement with my body. 'It's that way,' I said, and pointed through the Perspex into the darkness. I'd no idea what I was pointing at, but I knew he would not be able to resist turning to follow my arm.

He didn't. As he turned I stood up suddenly and threw myself at the sliding doors. I heard Bede say: 'Stop it, you fool,' but that was all. I had the lever in my hand and I went down on it. The panel slid open and Bede's hand was on my collar. I looked down at the ground, twelve feet below. The

Gazelle bucked suddenly, and I jumped. It was twelve feet and it felt like a hundred. As I fell I yelled out Sam's name and even as I hit the ground I heard a cry and a shot inside the hut. The corrugated iron reverberated as a bullet struck it and it was still ringing when the door burst open and Sam appeared and shouted: 'Run for it!'

Then I was on my feet and crossing the clearing in great leaps and the chopper was coming down on top of me and the spotlight whitewashed the earth and the air was filled with noise.

I heard three shots in those seconds, and before the third one had finished I was hurling myself at the doorway of the hut as if it was a paper hoop and before the bullet hit the doorframe I was through.

There was a lot going on inside but the scene etched itself on my retina in the split second I entered. The man Bede had called Dr Baker lay crumpled against one of the bunks like a discarded blanket, a pair of broken spectacles askew on his face. Elliott was flat against the wall by the fire, his hands high and an expression of pure terror on his face. Bill stood in front of him, a rifle in his hands. The barrel must have been sticking half-way through Elliott's abdomen. Both of them were breathing strenuously.

Sam had no part of this. He'd stepped aside from the doorway as I came through and when I was inside he stepped back again with a .303 at his shoulder.

He'd started firing before I had turned around again. 'Get your gun, mate,' he said, without turning. 'The window.'

I grabbed the SMLE and smashed the glass. Outside the Westland hovered like some huge night insect, its searchlight swaying to and fro in the darkness as it rocked.

I fired five times altogether and one of the shots hit the searchlight. There was a satisfying crash of broken glass and it went out. The machine began to rise unsteadily into the air. Sam stopped firing.

'They're more vulnerable than we are in those things,' he said. 'They may be able to hit any one of us – but one bullet in the right place and they all come down together. It won't be long before they think of a way to get back, though. Quickly, help me nobble these two. Put a few ropes round Baker.'

I knew what was going to happen to Elliott this time, so I didn't watch. I just heard the blow and the grunt, and then Sam said: 'Bill, put what we've got in that money-belt thing you wear. Grab as much gear as you can and put it in the pack. Then let's get out of here. I reckon we've got about five minutes.'

Looking back I think we used those five minutes very carefully. We hurled clothes, sleeping-bags, food and equipment into the packs while Bill wrapped cotton wool around a test tube, corked it, placed it inside a screw-top aluminium container, and put the container in his money belt.

On the floor Baker and Elliott groaned noisily. I threw the tea on the fire and it died in a cloud of smoke. Sam put the lamp out. 'Ready?' he said.

'Ready,' said Bill.

Outside, in the darkness, we could hear the Westland circling.

12 Running

We took a path behind the hut, past a pile of firewood and a primitive outhouse and into the trees. The track snaked up the ridge and we went with it. In ten minutes we had climbed out of the valley and the track led away to the left, along the ridge-top to the north. We ignored it. We followed the ridge south for another ten minutes and then began to descend on the other side.

The trees grew taller as we went down and within minutes we had been swallowed up by the forest and the night. It was hard even to hear the distant noise of the helicopter. The air was cool on our faces; there were dozens of small, unidentified movements in the undergrowth; and the black shapes of the trees fled past us in the darkness as though we were pushing our way through a throng of refugees leaving the scene of some disaster.

Soon we reached the bottom of the next valley, and where the stream broke the solidity of the forest we could see the sky, huge and pale overhead and jammed with stars. Sam plunged off up the stream southwards, and we followed him. It was only a few inches deep, clear and cold. Our boots crunched on the pebbles of its bed.

We plodded on for three-quarters of an hour, following the river's meandering as it grew smaller and the trees closed in about it. At last we came to an overhang of rock and beneath it a small beach of dry shingle. 'This'll do,' said Sam. We threw our packs on the ground and collapsed beside them. We unrolled our sleeping-bags and got in gratefully. 'Keep your clothes on and your boots nearby,' Sam said.

I lay back, stretched out and looked up through the black

shapes of the trees at the pale sky. High above, in the midst of a patch of starless space, a single star flashed and twinkled. There was no noise from the sky.

'I think a full explanation is overdue for our young friend,' said Bill. He turned to me. 'I could say to you that you have done your job for Lord Hammersham and you can set off out of here and return to England. But that would be hypocritical, wouldn't it? You're involved now. You are as much at risk as either of us, and if you tried to go back the way you came you would probably die in the attempt. I am truly sorry that my actions have brought you into this situation, but there it is. I can only apologize.'

I looked up into the Milky Way. He was right. I said: 'Before we were interrupted you said that what you recovered from the Cosmos was something that could be of immense importance to the human race. I assume that's what you brought with you. What is it? Why is it so important?'

'It is a source of food,' said Sam. 'A source of food which has never before been available to man.' He didn't turn towards me, just lay there on his back, talking into the night. 'There are one billion people on the planet suffering from malnutrition,' he said. 'Every year half a million of them die from starvation. What Bill has in that leather belt around his waist means simply this: those people will get food. Not just once but always. No more hunger.'

'Or it could mean that,' said Bill softly. 'If the military and the politicians keep their hands off it.'

'And that's where we come in?' I asked.

'That's where we come in,' said Sam. 'That's what this is all about.'

'Tell me,' I said, 'how the hell a fungus is going to feed a billion hungry people.'

The other dark shape spoke up. 'Very well,' said Bill. 'How much do you know about S C P? Single cell proteins?'

'Nothing,' I said.

'Right. I'll start at the beginning, then. Single cell protein is produced by single-celled animals: bacteria, yeasts, fungi, that sort of thing. Cattle eat grass, turn the grass into protein, we eat the cattle. It's exactly the same with the single cell creatures – except they have a considerably wider-ranging diet than cattle.

'The possibilities of farming single-celled animals didn't really emerge until after the last war, and strangely enough it was the petrochemical people who first came up with it. You don't think of oil refining being affected by the seasons, but it can be. A petroleum company had a problem with paraffin waxes in their crude oil. In winter the waxes hardened up and the oil didn't flow properly through the pipes – production slowed, profits fell. So they hired a very ingenious chap to work on it and he came up with a very ingenious solution. He discovered that a certain yeast by the name of candida absolutely thrives on paraffin waxes. Eats them like nobody's business: result, paraffin flows smoothly through the works. But there was a side effect: not only did candida eat the waxes, it grew fat on them. Given large amounts of nourishing waxes, candida dutifully produced large amounts of protein: edible protein.

'The petrol company was British Petroleum, and they knew a good thing when they saw one. Not only could they get rid of the paraffin waxes, they could also augment their profits by selling dried protein as cattle food. And by the sixties they were doing just that.

'Well, that was very useful. A small but valuable addition to the world's increasingly hard-pressed protein supplies. But, needless to say, petrol resources are in short supply themselves: it was hardly the answer to the world's food problem.

'There are, however, single-celled animals which have simpler tastes than candida, and it was the sugar people who found them. Their problem was waste. For every hundred tons of sugar cane you cut, eighty-seven have to be thrown away: human beings can't eat cane. So one of their chaps came up with the bright idea of getting single-celled animals to eat what human beings can't and turn it into protein.

'They struck lucky first by finding a customer for the husk of a bean known as the carob bean, of which they had more than they knew what to do with. The creature concerned went under the name of Aspergillus Niger, promptly shortened to MI. MI had the happy knack, when placed in a soup consisting of water and carob husk, of eating the sugar in the husks and turning it into protein. Within five hours it could double its own weight. Hey presto, more cattle feed.

'That's at the pilot plant stage now – in Central America. It's very useful, but it's still a complicated process needing quite a bit of investment and it still doesn't get to the heart of the possibilities for single cell protein. And I'll tell you why. You see, the bulk of the organic matter that plants create is not sugar, but cellulose. And cellulose is a form of carbohydrate which the human body is unable to use because we can't break it down. But there is a single-celled creature which can. A creature called Trichoderma Viride. Trichoderma Viride was first isolated feeding on a cotton cartridge belt in New Guinea towards the end of the last war. A cotton cartridge belt of course is pure cellulose, and it was finally discovered that the little creature was able to make a meal of such unpromising material because it produces an enzyme which is to cellulose as a flying brick is to a plate-glass window. Once smashed by this enzyme cellulose can be digested and turned into protein. One factor, however, held Trichoderma Viride back from a meteoric career: it is a fungus. And fungi are slow; they don't reproduce at anything like the rate of yeasts or bacteria. Put one of them on a pile of cellulose and you have a very long wait before you could invite anyone round to dinner.

'That's ordinary Trichoderma Viride. What came down in the Cosmos was a specimen which had mutated in an extraordinary way. First of all, it produces its enzyme at an incredibly high rate – so it can wolf through huge amounts of cellulose very swiftly. Secondly, it reproduces itself almost as fast as a yeast. And thirdly, it produces enough acids to effectively sterilize any medium it's working in. What that means is it can be used in very primitive conditions.'

'What do you mean, primitive conditions?' I said.

'Exactly where it's most needed. Imagine a village in India. They need feed for their animals. Even in the worst drought they can go out and gather up straw, grass, bits of twigs, anything made out of cellulose, and bring it back to the village and put it in, say, an oil drum. A specially converted oil drum, but, still, something cheap and easily available. All they would have to do is add liquid, a drop of a culture containing the Trichoderma Viride variant, and then wait. A few hours later they can filter the results, dry the powder and they have several pounds of straight single cell protein for their animals. It might even be safe for them to make it into some sort of soup and eat it themselves.

'Don't let this mislead you, of course,' Bill said. 'This isn't going to be possible next week. For a start we'll have to make sure the creature has stable reproduction patterns. We don't want it mutating into someting else straight away. Then it'll have to be tested, and not on just a few batches of animals, but on several generations of them to make sure it doesn't cause cancer or genetic malfunction or whatever. And then – or probably simultaneously – we'll have to develop economically viable techniques so that peasants can actually use it. But you can see, can't you, *why* it is so important?'

I could. It was no use saying I couldn't. In fact if you'd twisted my arm I would have had to admit that it was even important enough to justify the risks we were taking. But nobody twisted my arm. That answered the big intellectual questions; it only left the equally large practical ones.

'I take your point about me being involved now,' I said. 'Consider me as one of the party. So what's the party going to do next?'

'Get the hell out of here,' said Sam. 'Get out of here and get this thing into the hands of the people who can develop it. Bill knows most of them personally. We want to get down to the Department of Scientific and Industrial Research in Wellington, produce a few cultures, and send them off to these guys. That way nobody'll be able to suppress it, pervert it to their own ends, use it as a weapon, whatever.'

'You can see how it would be a very good thing if scientists from the Third World itself were able to get the variant into production,' Bill said. 'Professor Varky in Bombay springs to mind. He would make a splendid job of it. There are several others. The first step is to get down to the D S I R in Wellington and start distributing it.'

'There'll be a little opposition to that, won't there?' I said. I didn't want to sound pessimistic, but the way Bill was talking, Wellington lay half a mile down the road, and even the little geography of the country that I had gathered told me it lay a long way away from where we were that night. I went on: 'We had a visit from the Americans tonight; it can't be long before they find the Cosmos and when they do they're going to realize it's been looted. We're going to be prime suspects, aren't we? They've taken a lot of trouble to find that thing – I can't see them just leaving it at that. And I can't see Karyanin and the K G B allowing us to walk off with their bugs, whether they know one of them is a world beater or not. They're going to come in here after us. How do we get from here to Wellington without being waylaid, robbed and probably killed on the way by the C I A, the K G B, or both?'

'We walk and keep our heads down,' said Sam. 'The ranges we're in are very rough country; when you're lost in them you're very hard to find. When you want to lose yourself in them you're almost invisible. If we turn around and walk out towards the east coast, there's a reasonable chance they won't be able to find us.'

'Why the east coast?' I asked. 'Wellington's south of here, isn't it?'

'The ranges run north and south,' Sam said. 'They run the entire length of the island and, generally speaking, are uninhabited: they're too wild. It would take a very long time to get right down the length of the island through terrain like this. But if we can cross the ranges eastwards, we'll come out in Hawke's Bay, sheep country. There's an airport there, trains, roads, the lot. We should be able to make it from there without too much trouble . . .' He paused. 'But it's not going to be easy. As I say, it's very hard to find people here, but it's equally hard for people to find themselves. It's bloody hard work, just surviving. We've got about five days' worth of food with us, and that should do it. With luck. We've got maps for the next ten, twenty miles, depending which route we pick. After that it'll be a matter of relying on the sun and the compass. And all the time we'll be slogging our way up and down the meanest damn mountains you ever came across in your life. Has anybody got a better plan?'

Nobody had. 'All right,' said Bill. 'Okay,' I said. 'Start at dawn,' said Sam.

And that was that.

I lay there, thinking and staring out into space, and the last thing I remember hearing is the sound of the stream running over the stones.

We woke at six the next morning, and there was a layer of mist, six inches deep, hanging over the stream. The sky looked like skies ought always to look, and through the morning chill there was the promise of warmth to come. It was the sort of day which, when you are trapped in asphalt streets between brick walls, awakens deep primitive lusts to move, to leave behind the safe and familiar, and to set out somewhere.

We washed ourselves in the icy stream, plunging our hands through the mist and watching them disappear as if they were entering another dimension. We ate a light breakfast, replaced the rolled sleeping-bags in the packs, and set off. We left the stream and climbed up out of its valley and on to another of the hog's-back ridges. We went south with it for an hour or so and then went down a spur till we came to a broad valley with a river sufficiently substantial to have banks we could walk along.

It was early yet and there was no sign of any activity in the sky. We followed the river south until it became too deep to wade and its banks too steep to use. Gradually we were forced higher up the side of the valley until the river lay a hundred feet below us, and with every dozen yards the incline became steeper. Soon we were hauling ourselves along on roots and creepers and the sodden earth gave way beneath our boots. Great clumps of it went curving away through the air down to the bottom of the gorge.

Towards mid-morning we came out at the end of the valley, where the ridge dropped straight down for two hundred feet, and to our left the river poured out over a lip of rock and plunged down with it, forming a rainbow in the morning sun. It looked like a stream of molten metal; some ore so rare its very existence spanned no more than the time it took to fall to the bottom of the cliff.

Across the gorge the ranges lay piled like a furious green sea frozen at the height of an ancient storm. We sat down on mossy logs and studied the remaining miles of terrain for which the map could guide us.

The sky was still empty.

It took us three-quarters of an hour to find a route down the cliff and reach the other side of the gorge, and as noon passed we slogged our way diagonally up the valley wall on the other side.

'I suppose it's no use sticking to the rivers because they generally flow north and south with the ranges?' I asked Sam, during a break.

'Right, generally. Some of them do flow east-west, but the problem is they meander. If you followed them it could take you weeks to get out; they're about as straight as a heap of string. No, the best way to travel in this country is on the ridge-tops. You can get some idea where you're going and it's generally easier walking. Unfortunately, you can't stay on the ridge-tops all the time because they're too tangled as well. So it's a matter of going with them as far as you can and climbing on to another that's going in the direction you want to go when yours won't take you any farther.

'If you're totally lost, though, you can fall back on the streams and rivers. They may take a long time but they will ultimately get you out. Little streams flow into bigger streams and bigger streams flow into rivers and rivers flow down to the coast. There's a settlement within reach of most coastal areas in New Zealand. So, if you're bushed, don't panic, find a stream.' He grinned encouragingly. 'But stick with us and it won't happen.'

We rested when we reached the top, and lay with our backs on the warm earth. I looked up through the soft green fronds of the ferns, along the endless, branchless boles of the rimus and finally through the canopy of foliage up above.

Bill dug out some matches and tobacco and lit his pipe with a sigh of contentment. Sam lay against the trunk of a beech, his face dark, thinking. I let my muscles relax and watched the depths of blue that appeared through the green when a breeze shifted the distant branches. The air was still and hot. We gave ourselves twenty minutes.

The rest of the afternoon was fairly easy going. Once, I thought I heard the noise of a helicopter, but it was right on the edge of hearing, far away, and by the time we reached a spot where we could see the sky it was gone. Bill talked as we went, about the forest through which we were travelling, about its moods and its rhythms. He talked about his work in the days of the green revolution, about what they had been doing at Hinaki. But principally he talked about the variant and all his hopes for it. All that it would end and all that it would begin. All that he would do to make sure it became what he knew it could become. He was absorbed in his vision, inspired by it. Listening to him, I suddenly felt how vulnerable and weak we were and how great the odds against us, not least the bush itself, but somehow I felt we would come through. And there seemed to be no incongruity in the spectacle of a fat middle-aged man labouring through vicious terrain, hunted by the agents of the two most powerful nations in the world, with the possible food supply for millions of starving people belted between the folds of fat on his belly.

At last the sun began to go down in a haze of pale grey clouds streaked with livid pink, and we climbed down off the ridge before it began to twist away westward. Sam urged us on to one last effort. We filled our water bottles at the stream, crossed the valley, and made it up the other side before collapsing exhausted for the night. The forest filled up with darkness, we ate, stretched ourselves out, and slept.

*

Next morning we heard it straight away, but we couldn't see it, and by the time we had dashed to a knoll clear of trees the sky seemed empty again. But there was no mistaking that sound. It was the helicopter. And it was close.

We went back to the camp, quickly grabbed something to eat, slung the packs on our backs and set off. There is always a slightly empty, sick feeling when you start tramping early in the morning, but that day it was worse. We were all still half asleep, dazed and stiff. We marched woodenly along the ridge-back, the thick green canopy above our heads, and above that, now nearer, now farther away, the sound of the chopper.

It felt as though a lid had been clamped on the sky.

After an hour it went away, but nobody said anything because nobody believed it had gone for long. And nobody was wrong. It came back towards eleven, and this time we saw it from a long way off, red and white against the rich blue sky. And when I saw it, a cold sliver of fear melted suddenly and trickled down my spine.

It wasn't the Westland. It was another sort of helicopter. It was called a Sikorsky.

There were three possible explanations for its appearance. One was that the Westland had been damaged worse than we'd thought in last night's fire-fight, and had had to be replaced. The second was that the Americans had simply augmented it with a second chopper, for good measure. The third was that the K G B had moved into the business of hunting by heli-copter as well.

I had an unpleasant feeling that this last possibility was the one to put your money on. I was right.

We heard the Sikorsky at intervals for the next hour or two, steadily quartering every square mile of country for perhaps two or three miles around. It did not seem to concentrate on the ridges and valleys around us. Whenever we came to a stretch of ridge where the trees were thin we headed down the slope and hacked our way, doubled up and unseen, through the bush lawyer and creepers on the forest floor.

We lunched at one, in a deep dim green dip in the ridge, the canopy so thick overhead it closed off the sky entirely.

The Sikorsky flew over us, no more than five or six feet above the tree-tops, before we were half-way through.

There had been no warning: some freak of the landscape must have killed the noise of their engines till they were above us, and we were all unnerved, shocked into immobility as though we had been caught in a searchlight. When it had gone, we all agreed it was a freak of chance, that it meant nothing, that they couldn't possibly have known we were there. But for the first time I began to feel hunted.

We did not stay there long after that. We pushed on. During the afternoon there was no further sign of the Sikorsky, although occasionally we caught a distant buzz of its engines.

We swopped ridges at about two, upped and downed a little over some jumbled country, and made it up to another good hog's-back about four. 'That's about how far the map can take us,' said Sam, squatting down with the compass a little while later. 'From now on we rely on this and our own good judgement. With a bit of luck it'll be another two or three days.'

'Good,' said Bill. Lines of fatigue were beginning to show on his face: but that was all.

We walked long into the evening. Although there was no track as such, the going was surprisingly easy and the route clear of obstacles: all we had to do was stick to the top of the ridge. After the heat of the day the gradual cooling of evening was a relief, and somehow it seemed easier to keep going than to make the decision to stop.

There was no noise in the darkness except the noise of the forest creatures. It was good. About nine o'clock the ridge dipped into a hollow filled with a mass of dry, dead fern. The trees were thick above us, the hollow deep and secure and the ferns made a soft, comfortable mattress. We unrolled our sleeping-bags, ate a handful of dried fruit each, and went straight into a deep sleep.

They arrived at about two in the morning.

13   The Night Visitors

There was something in my dreams, burrowing underground, deep down, and as it burrowed the earth above it shifted, and suddenly the dream was full of unease, and I woke.

A yard away a dark, kneeling figure was going through my pack. He had his back to me, bent over, and he was steadily removing each item from the pack and examining it by the light of a tiny pencil-torch.

I didn't make any sound, any indication that I was awake; I just watched him for a few moments, then reached over silently to where Sam lay in his sleeping-bag, and dug him sharply in the ribs. I put my hand over his mouth and he understood; he woke silently. I sensed his eyes opening and focusing and seeing the man. I could almost hear the tiny sharp intake of breath. Then he made a slight movement with his head. I understood.

I shifted gently in the sleeping-bag, easing myself into a position where it would fall from me as I leapt, and I knew Sam was doing the same. The searcher was still intent on his search. I was ready.

We both sprang together, and hit the man almost simultaneously. I never found out what it felt like for Sam, but for me it felt like taking a running jump at the Great Pyramid. The man dived forward as we hit him and in one movement swept round and landed me a solid roundhouse right on the jaw. Then he and Sam rose together out of the vegetation like two prehistoric monsters batling in some primeval swamp, and if the fight had gone on it would have been something to see. It lasted about twenty seconds. Karyanin stopped it. His voice rasped out of the darkness and we spun round at the sound of it. And froze.

Encircling the hollow, silent and immobile as statues, stood a ring of men. Even in the darkness it was clear that each held a rifle. And Karyanin was in charge.

'Well met, my friends,' he said, stepping forward and flicking on a torch. He shone it straight into our faces. I couldn't see his expression, but I didn't need to. I could imagine the smile working on those thin, red lips. I could imagine it very well.

'Well met,' he repeated, savouring the words. 'There's no need for explanations and none, certainly, for heroics, as you see. You have had, as you say, a run for your money, and are now faced with superior numbers. Will you hand over what you have stolen, please? Immediately!'

The shock wore off, and cold replaced it, working outwards from the gut. I opened my mouth to say something, and couldn't. There was no saliva there, and my tongue stuck to the palate. My eyes were fixed on Karyanin's like a bird hypnotized by a snake.

Then Sam spoke. I could hear the hatred in his voice. It was low and hoarse, and Karyanin had to make him repeat what he had said.

'In my pack, at the bottom, inside two bags of sugar. Just tip it out.'

Karyanin must have translated his words verbatim, without thinking, because the searcher strode to where Sam's pack lay and emptied it into the ferns.

It was a mistake, and I heard Karyanin bite his teeth together as he realized it, but he didn't say anything. As the clothes, maps, toilet gear and food cascaded out into the undergrowth, I tore my eyes from the torch and glanced at Sam to acknowledge his tiny victory. Down in the ferns I could see his feet moving.

He was slipping his boots on. I followed suit. Karyanin said something and two of the men from the ring put their guns down and came forward to help with the search. They went through everything, slitting open bags and letting the contents run through their fingers, methodically slicing every piece of clothing. A little circle of devastation spread in the darkness around them.

I noticed, as they worked, that they were all convincingly dressed as trampers, in check bush shirts, oilskin parkas and shorts. In any other circumstances they would have seemed a perfectly innocent party of overseas visitors. It was only here, for us, that they appeared for what they were. Or what they would be, once they found what they were looking for. A firing squad.

Now the pack was finished. Piles of sugar, dried fruit, heaps of rags and tatters of maps lay in the ferns like the aftermath of a wild picnic. They looked at what they had done for a moment, and then sliced up the pack. They took the frame to pieces and checked inside each piece of tubing. There was nothing.

Everything was silent for a moment; all of us, the troopers and Sam and I, looking at Karyanin to see what he would do. I saw, even in the darkness, a little ripple of fury cross his face. He controlled it, turned and stepped over to Sam.

He swung the torch into Sam's face with an impact I can still almost feel now. 'You are a fool,' he said, and before the words were out of his mouth he hit him again. Sam grunted.

My stomach began to contract steadily and, it seemed, endlessly. When it had reached minimum size, like the inside of a golf ball, it began to descend slowly through my abdominal cavity.

Far off in the bush an animal cried out; a sudden, curtailed shriek as some creature of prey took it. I felt for it.

It was then that I saw, out of the corner of my eye, a furtive movement down in the darkness, and I realized, with a jolt, that they had forgotten all about Bill.

In fact they probably knew nothing about Bill. Karyanin had seen me and he had seen Sam. However they had got on to us during the previous day, they hadn't had a chance for a good, long look.

They did not know that Bill was with us. And in the deep disguise of the ferns they had not seen him yet. But what the hell was Bill going to be able to do against this lot?

Sam started to say something, and before he got it out Karyanin hit him again. 'Don't lie,' he said. I wondered when he was going to start on me.

Sam started speaking again, but I didn't listen to what he was saying. I listened instead to a tiny sound coming from where Bill lay in his sleeping-bag. It was the sound of something being emptied from a bottle. After it came a tiny rattle. It was then that I guessed.

'Karyanin,' I said, 'I think I can help you.' There was only one reason for speaking, and that was to make a noise. It was noise Bill needed now, to cover the sound he had to make. Karyanin turned to me and as he turned it happened. It happened a damn sight faster than any of us had any right to expect.

The hollow exploded into flame. It went up like a bonfire. It went up like a bomb. It saved us.

Bill had two weapons within his reach when he woke up and realized what was going on. They were a bottle of lighter fluid and a tube of matches. He thought fast and worked even faster. He emptied a trail of lighter fluid as far from him as he could manage, soaking the dry, dead ferns. Then he took his handkerchief and stuffed it in the neck of the half-empty bottle, roughly as prescribed by Molotov. It was at that point he needed me to cover the noise of the match being struck. The Molotov cocktail he hurled quite silently.

The amount of flammable material in that hollow was quite amazing. The ferns, for a start. They were like a great mass of tinder, and they needed only the smallest amount of encouragement to go up. The wrecked contents of the pack provided a good deal of that encouragement. The rags. The paper. The sugar. And, of course, a bottle of lighter fluid. And seconds after the cocktail exploded into a raging inferno of vegetation, there were two more explosions. They were the aerosol cans of insect repellent. We hadn't packed them; they were there by chance, because they had been in the packs when Bill and Sam grabbed them two nights before. They tipped the scales.

Karyanin's first reaction when the hollow went up was one of pure amazement. I don't blame him. He had both of us, Sam and I, in front of him, and there was no way either of us could have done it. There seemed no way anyone could have done it in that brief fraction of a second. There was no immediate enemy to attack. So he grabbed me. He took one stride and took me by the shirt and hauled me straight up.

That was when the can exploded. I don't know how many pieces of metal embedded themselves in his back but there must have been quite a few of them. He screamed loudly straight into my face and dropped me. Then a great gout of flame sprang up between us and I leapt backwards. Sam disappeared. Bill disappeared. There was nothing except smoke, flames and noise. I began to feel my way up the banks of the hollow, and the smell of burning hair filled my nostrils. It was my own.

It was then, of course, that they should have gunned us down; and if they had been able to see us they would have done it. But Karyanin was in the hollow. And in that inferno anyone could have been anyone else. So we clawed our way out of the hollow and ran.

How I avoided hitting anything I shall never know, because I went along that black-forested ridge-top as if I had been on a 440 track, out in front, and when the firing started the bullets whined past and smacked into the tree trunks as though they were me.

Sam and Bill were ahead, and as I caught up I could hear Bill breathing like a pair of bellows with a hole in them. I didn't have the breath to spare, but I still said it as I came up to them. 'You beauty, Bill. You beauty'; and then we were all pounding along together and we could hear them behind us, shouting and firing as they ran.

'To the left here, mates,' said Sam, and we crashed off the ridge-top and began ploughing down through the thick undergrowth of the slope. It was pitch black. The slope increased with every yard until it felt like running down the side of a lighthouse. And suddenly, seconds later, there was nothing there, and the roots of the creepers were ripping out of the earth under our weight, and we plunged straight down into the blackness.

It felt as if the whole ridge was falling away, but it wasn't. All that had happened was that we had stepped over the edge of a thirty-foot cliff, and if it had not been for the fact that the undergrowth flowed over its edge and down its entire face like the overflow of a boiling cauldron, we would have gone straight down and lain there, broken, until the men from the K G B came to take us.

As it was, the cliff was the next link in the chain that kept us from them that night.

The wall of creepers swung away from the ridge and we went down with it, flailing about in the darkness until the whole curtain piled on to the canopy of the trees below, and we slithered off, tearing and grasping at the trunks and branches as we fell, crashing to a halt at their feet, bruised, winded and unhurt.

Above us, silhouetted against the blazing forest, stood the Russians. And the fastest of them did not stop. He leapt straight on, coming down after us.

The snap when his neck broke stays with me to this hour. There was no cry, just that noise. No one else on the cliff-top moved. We slid away into the night and began to run. Behind us the smoke billowed into a sky glowing red from the fire.

They started firing again then, but it was too late and they knew it. All they could do was follow us on the ridge-top as we ran down the valley; and that was what they did.

The valley itself sloped steeply, and that was good, because with every yard we ran the ridge rose higher on our right, and the cliff that kept our pursuers from us grew more impassable. We could follow their progress from the occasional flashes of rifle fire, but for them we must have been invisible. Soon the flaming ridge-top disappeared behind us, and there was only the smell of burning wood on the breeze.

The valley felt like a rat run. It was steep and narrow and the stream-bed was full of harsh, broken rocks. We ran on and on down its length as if it was one of those mazes they make small animals run through in laboratories. At any moment the shutter would come down and they would switch the current on. End of experiment. It must have been because I had not woken up properly yet.

The valley did end abruptly, spilling out into the broad path of a major river. There was a great sweeping slope down to the water, the trees thick as though they had gathered to applaud the river's progress, and even at the mouth of the tributary valley we could hear its roaring. It was larger than any river we had yet met.

'Upstream or downstream?' I said, and Sam replied: 'Across it. We've got to get it between us and them. They'll never think we'd tackle it at night. Okay, Bill?'

'Okay, old son,' said Bill. It took him a while to get it out. Listening to him breathe was like listening to a ripsaw going through a pile of scrap metal. But while he had it in him, he was game for anything. 'Okay, old son,' he said.

And we made our way through the trees down to the river.

The forest ended abruptly, and we began to stumble over the boulders which the river had thrown up as it went. Suddenly the water stretched away in front of us, silvery in the starlight, roaring like a maniac.

It was too dark to see the other side.

Beneath its roar, we could hear the boulders crashing and grinding against each other. We stopped. We were all of us shocked by the ferocity of what lay before us. It was not what we had expected. Behind us, a quarter of a mile away on the bluff where the ridge ended, one of the Russians must have thought he saw something, because a shot rang out and a ragged volley followed it.

We glanced at each other and nodded. 'Link arms,' said Sam, and we did. Bill was in the middle. We walked over the shingle and straight into the water, without stopping. We went straight into the river and the water rose to our calves, to our knees, to our waists.

It was like stepping into a refrigerated coffin. The water filled my boots and I felt warmth and then feeling gradually drain out of my feet. The stones, rolled along the river-bed by the water, pounded into my legs and then rolled on past, leaving them bruised and bleeding. With every step the river became deeper, and the water rose from my waist up to my chest, and its strength grew as it rose. It ceased to feel like water. It felt like treacle, like quicksand, like a flow of freezing lava. I actually made those wild comparisons out there, in mid-river, forcing myself to think rationally, not to give way to the panic.

With every step the river grew deeper.

We had taken on more than we realized. We had been thrown, by our terror, into a venture that could only be suicidal. We had saved ourselves from the K G B only to throw our lives to the river. We would never be able to reach the other side.

The darkness terrified me as much as anything. As the water rose towards my neck and the lava solidified about me the darkness suddenly became very important. I could not see. All that lay ahead was a surge of water and shadows. I was walking from darkness to darkness. Every step seemed to be the last.

When we lifted each foot from its place to make the next step the river took hold of the leg and waved it, like the boneless limb of some sea-plant, and we had to force each ounce of will to bear on the empty muscles to bring the foot down again and step onwards.

And with each step we sank deeper. Bill's arm, locked with mine at the elbow, tightened its grip as we went down. The river roared in my ears as though the universe was sluicing down a vortex. I forced my foot down in another step. No deeper, please. For Christ's sake let it be no deeper. I forced the panic back again and spat the water away from my mouth. I could feel the river around me, ready to make the last assault, ready to tip the balance and lift us off our feet in the darkness to sweep us away and smash us as it smashed boulders.

I pushed my foot down again. It was horribly slow, it took an eternity to thrust its way through that solid water and back to the river-bed. And when it reached it the descent had stopped. It was no deeper. No deeper. We would make it.

It was then that Bill gave way. I felt him stumble and lose his footing, and gasped at the tremendous drag on my arm as the river took him. We hauled him upright again, but he had no time to steady himself and this time, as he went, cannoning into Sam, he dragged me with him and my boots slid on the stones, downstream. We were being carried away. The river would have us after all.

I dug my feet into the river-bed, screwed them into the stones with everything I had in me, and leant away from Bill into the current. It tore at us as the wind tears at a sail, and my boots ploughed through the gravelly bottom like blades. Then Sam must have gained a purchase somewhere and we stopped moving. We teetered there, in mid-stream, struggling silently with the current.

I don't know how long it lasted, but it seemed to be for ever, and there seemed to be no way forward, just endless effort and oblivion at the end of it. Then I felt Bill take an iron grip on himself, and he said something inaudible, and he was moving again, and we went with him, dragging huge concrete blocks of weariness behind us.

Gradually the far bank came nearer, and every yard took us into shallower water, until the current was no more than a hammering at our knees; and then we were out of it, stumbling on to the shingle of the far bank, coughing and whooping, staggering forward to drop.

'No!' said Sam. 'Can't yet. Get into the trees first, quickly!' We just managed to reach them. Nobody turned round to look back across the river, we just tottered into the black forest edges and collapsed. When I opened my eyes – it could have been minutes, could have been hours later – the first thing that caught them was the fire. Immensely distant, it seemed, over the water and far into the hills. The sky above it glowed like a warning light. I stared at the fire and as I stared I remembered what it was and how it came to be lit. I turned and shook Sam and Bill and managed to make it to my feet.

I slumped against a tree trunk. I felt like an old man. I also felt as if I had just climbed out of a spin dryer.

We went downstream then, because Sam still had the compass and that was the direction it told us to go. We followed him because we were too exhausted to argue. He told us what to do in brief, staccato phrases, because he had no strength for anything else. He told us that we had to get farther away before we could rest, because in the morning they would cross the river, in case we had come that way, and if we were near they would find us. We had to find another tributary, follow its valley until it hid us, and then we could rest. And it could not be the first one. They would search that.

We set off downstream through the undergrowth while alongside us the river roared dimly.

Do you remember how they once used to give away little plastic toys in cereal packets? Animals, with legs that moved. You tied a piece of cotton to them, put a weight on the end of the cotton, and hung it over the edge of a table. Pulled by the weight the little plastic animal tottered to the edge of the table and stopped; or went over, as the case may be. It was in a like manner that we tottered along the riverbank that night.

It took us twenty minutes before we splashed through the first tributary, and half an hour before we came to the next, and at each Sam shook his head and we passed them by, and still nobody argued. But we stopped not long after that, slumping against the trees. Sam and I stayed close to Bill because we were afraid that if we did not he would fall. Bill wasn't saying anything now; he wasn't complaining, wasn't demanding rest. He was concentrating all his energies into putting one foot before the other. As it had felt for me, in the middle of the river, it must have felt for him for most of that last stretch that night. He lay against his tree as if he had been nailed there. And all the time, like poison working its way through the system, the fact sank into me that we had lost almost everything. We had lost our packs, our food, medicine, spare clothing, sleeping-bags, maps, guns. We were sodden and exhausted, bruised, stripped and hunted like animals. We were in the middle of a vicious and all but impenetrable expanse of forest and mountains and every one of them demanded more energy and strength than any of us had left. The fact that we carried hope for half the world didn't mean a thing.

I suspect it was only the rifle-shots that got us moving again. I'd drifted off, swirling with the currents of sleep, and it was the shots that woke me. They were far away, across the river, but they were enough. We set off again.

It was nearly forty minutes before we came to the next stream, and when we reached it Sam said: 'All right, this'll do.' And we splashed up it and into the valley from which it flowed. It was a tiny stream, just a few inches deep, and its valley was no more than a gash in the mountains. But it was a deep, steep gash for all that, solid with bush lawyer and tree ferns and every kind of vegetation. Soon the stream grew too narrow to use as a highway, and we hauled ourselves along through the wet greenery of the valley-sides with the listlessness of exhaustion. We ended up crawling on our hands and knees, worming our way into the heart of the valley, into the anonymity of that dense mass of living stuff.

Finally we came to a fallen beech log across our path, no more than ten feet long and two or three feet high. It looked like the Berlin Wall. We stopped. Bill began to sleep immediately.

'Okay,' said Sam, and staggered to his feet. He began to tear off the fronds from the tree ferns, piling them on the ground beside us. I levered myself up and followed suit mechanically, and when we had a pile large enough we rolled Bill into it and crawled in ourselves. We pulled the few remaining fronds over our heads. Then we slept.

During the night it began to rain.

The heap of fronds was just far enough from my eyes to be able to focus on them; droplets of last night's rain hung from the green feathers like glass beads. As I watched they shivered ecstatically, released their hold and fell gently on to my face. Far above, through the branches, the sky was the colour of lead.

Bill lay a few feet away, his mouth open, his face naked and shapeless without his glasses. He looked like an old man. I could hear Sam moving about somewhere a little way off. I looked back at the sky again.

I turned it blue, to start with. When the sky is that sort of blue it becomes so deep that you think you are looking into a still, deep pool. Then I drew the sun towards me, and it poured into the valley like wine and seeped into my body through every pore. It dried the ferns and each branch of the trees and the dry smells of the hot forest began to fill the air. I lay there, looking up through the leaves into the vault of heaven and the day drifted by. A few minutes later Sam came back, with breakfast. He held his hands cupped together, squatting in front of us grinning proudly till Bill woke. 'Tucker,' he whispered, and opened his hands. Six large white grubs squirmed in his palm. 'Huhu grubs. See the dark brown heads? Bite them off and spit them out. Eat the rest. Go on – it should taste something like peanut butter. Very nutritious.' And he thrust them at us.

We looked at them for a moment, watched Sam eat one, and then tried for ourselves. They did taste slightly like peanut butter. Slightly.

'Lesson number one,' Sam said. 'You can live off the land.

You don't have to have guns and you don't have to have supplies. There's plenty of water round to drink. So cheer up, you mournful bastards. You look as if you've just been to a funeral. In fact, just to give you a real thrill, here's your second course. It's not as good as the first course, actually, because you should cook it, but it's very nutritious as well and it'll be very filling.' And he handed us each a couple of fern shoots.

It was impossible not to smile at Sam's enthusiasm, particularly when we tried to eat the shoots. They tasted like a handful of very tough grass. But filling: nobody needed to eat a second one.

Bill said: 'All right, touch wood, let's congratulate ourselves. We shouldn't have got this far intact and we have. Our chances of getting the rest of the way intact are just as slim but we'll give it a bloody good go, as Sam would put it. How far do you think we've got, Sam?'

'It's hard to say. I reckon a couple of days should see us through to the edge of the sheep country in Hawke's Bay, if we don't get lost. We're relying on the compass and common sense now, remember. Give us a few minutes while I try to work out which direction we should be going from here.' He cleared a patch of earth and scratched in it with one of the uneaten shoots. After a few minutes he said: 'I think up to the top of this valley; it should take us on to a spur at least, possibly a main ridge. According to me that'll be the direction we want to go, but we'll check with the compass when we get there.'

'What about our Slavic friends?' I said. 'Even if they couldn't find us last night they must have realized roughly how far we could get. They'll be doing this area pretty thoroughly, I should imagine.'

'Well, that's where crossing the river helps,' said Sam. 'They can't be certain whether we've done it, so they'll have to search both sides. I didn't gather how many of them there were last night, but it wasn't more than a dozen, probably less. If I were them I'd guard the exits, the best ridges for getting out of the area. So we've got to get there before they do.'

'Don't forget the helicopters,' said Bill. 'That lot were dropped in last night: they didn't just follow us. The helicopters will be back, I'm afraid.'

'Let's worry about that when it happens,' I said. 'I don't know about you lot, but I'm ready for off. These clothes are too damned wet to hang about in.' There was no dispute.

We washed in the trickle of a stream, and began to stumble and haul ourselves up between the walls of the valley. All the rain that had lodged in the foliage the night before was dislodged again as we passed, completing its inevitable journey back to the surface of the planet. It was like walking through a swimming pool. The sky was still like lead.

As we went, each of us thought to himself about what Bill had said that night so long ago when we had packed our things and fled from the hut while the helicopter circled overhead.

'From our point of view,' he had said, 'the bush and the mountains are advantageous to the extent that they make us very hard to find.' I unreeled the hours of steady, sunlit tramping, while the helicopters cruised fruitlessly above the forest and we had packs on our backs and rifles. And suddenly, superimposed on this, was Karyanin's face, torchlit in the darkness of the clearing, and then the cocktail exploded, and he screamed at me, and I was running, running like an idiot through the darkness, while the bullets killed the trees around me.

'From the point of view of our pursuers,' Bill had said, 'the same environment is advantageous because it allows them to do almost what they like. If they can find us.'

They had found us. The balance of advantage had tipped, and now the bush was a trap and not an escape route. And beyond that, it was a killer in itself. Because whatever Sam said, without proper food, dry clothes and sleeping-bags, this country would kill us. And we all knew it. It was just a matter of time.

It took us forty minutes to make our way out of that cleft in the mountains, and when we had done it we found that the effort had taken us to no more than the spur of a minor ridge.

Dimly, through the clouds that draped themselves like vacant shrouds over the forest, we could see the sweep of mountain up ahead.

'That's the range we want,' said Sam. 'It takes us south-east, and that's the way we've got to go.' It looked a long way, and it was.

It would have been hard work if we had been rested, dry and well fed on the first day of an expedition. Wet, hungry, sleepless, bruised and exhausted, it was hell. After that first glimpse the forest thickened again and there was nothing to see except the great smooth trunks rising into the rain, and the rich green undersea world of the forest. There was nothing to do except climb.

The best part of the morning had passed when we reached the junction of ridge and mountain, and when we reached it we sank quietly to the ground among the undergrowth and nobody said anything.

The two Russians stood in the perfect strategic spot to watch and control everything that happened in a large circle around them. They could guard our ridge, the main range, and another spur that we might have been using. They had rifles and binoculars and a walkie-talkie. They were our full stop.

If we had been in good physical shape we would have taken it better, but we weren't in good shape, and we were thoroughly demoralized. We lay in the damp gloom and signalled suggestions to each other and each of them was rejected as it was made. They were too vigilant to rush and we were too weak. They had too clear a field of vision to try crawling up to the path through the undergrowth. They were too well positioned to leave the spot until somebody told them to: and nobody would tell them to until we were found.

And we were too exhausted to go back the way we had come. Even if we had been able to.

We just lay there, in miserable, unthinking lethargy and waited while the damp and chill percolated through us.

We waited for an hour. At the end of an hour the helicopter

arrived. It was the moment when they say, 'Our hearts sank.' What they should say is, 'Our guts contracted and shivers ran through various unexpected places.' Something like that. The bastards. The sentries had seen us. They had kept their cool. They had raised Karyanin and they had not let on. Now the rest of the boys had arrived for the fun. And they had arrived to take us. Bastards.

Then we recognized the sound of the engine. It wasn't the Sikorsky at all. It was the Westland Gazelle. The Americans were back. The Americans were flying past.

And the two Russians were very interested indeed. One of them spoke urgently into the walkie-talkie and the other focused the binoculars on the Westland. As they spoke and watched, they moved unthinkingly to a spot where they could see the chopper clearly.

It wasn't far, it was no more than ten or fifteen yards. But it was enough.

We started to crawl.

The worst part was that we could not see them. Once we had put our heads down among the undergrowth there was no raising them. We just had to crawl up the path and hope. It felt like crawling past a buzz-saw with your eyes closed.

The last few yards were almost vertical and every snap of a root sounded like a dozen Christmas crackers. I was the last to make the climb, and when I slid on to the ridge my heart stopped. The sentries were about twenty feet away. They were still absorbed by the Westland. We looked at each other. Right? Right.

We stood up, braced ourselves for the impact of their bullets, and walked across the open ground that separated us.

They did not turn. We slipped into the trees and turned left. The range was ours. We had made it. The road to the south lay before us. It only remained to traverse it.

For two hours we did just that. The compass said we were going in the right direction, and we simply followed the ridge. It dipped and climbed and veered occasionally one way or another, but it didn't matter. All it required of us was that we followed it. At about one-thirty Sam dug about in the earth and I combed a rotten log for more huhu grubs and we scraped together a semblance of a midday meal. I don't remember enjoying it but it was good for morale. After that the route was steeper and we had to work harder.

About mid-afternoon we came out on a small peak where a giant rimu had collapsed, taking half a dozen smaller trees with it. There was a view and we looked at it.

It looked almost exactly like every other panorama we had seen in four days in the bush. The country was vicious and tangled and steep and the carpet of forest was unbroken. This time we were higher than we had been yet and most of it lay below us, pasted with grey clouds. Clouds hid much of the range that lay ahead, too.

It didn't hide the flash of colour less than a mile behind us. It didn't hide the fact that the flash repeated itself very quickly a few yards farther through the trees. It didn't hide the fact that the Russians were on the ridge and following us. It didn't hide the fact that the Russians were following us very fast indeed. They knew we had broken through the net.

It didn't hide the Westland either. The Westland was a long way off. But as I watched it I knew that if the Russians did not catch us, the people in the Westland would.

Or ... they might catch each other. The thought surfaced urgently as if it had been struggling up through the depths of my mind for a long time, trying to reach the air.

'Bill, have you looked in your pocket for your matches? You had them in an aluminium container in your shirt pocket. Did you use them all last night? Did you lose them?'

'No, old son, didn't lose them. Here they are, all safe and dry. But we can't light a fire, can we?'

'There may be an advantage to it,' I said, and explained what I had in mind. Bill smiled and Sam nodded. We began to tear broken branches from the dead rimu. Sam shredded the twigs into kindling. Bill found a rotten log and pulled off the wet outer layers until he found the dry, dusty heart within. We piled them all together. We lit them.

The tiny yellow flame took hold and the twigs blackened and burnt. The rotten wood began to catch and the branches above it to steam dry. We hauled green branches off living trees and propped them above the heap. They would burn later.

Then we turned to go. It was an effort, tiny as the fire was, to leave. It was a jewel in that dark, dripping place and its miniature warmth was a home.

'That should fetch them,' said Sam.

The trees closed in about us once more.

As we walked I drew them towards each other, as I had drawn the sun up that morning. But this was real. Far down the ridge the Russians sniffed the breeze. They looked at each other and nodded. And their pace quickened. In the Westland Murdoch reached for the binoculars, focused them, and smiled. He turned to Bede and said something. Bede picked up his rifle. Elliott adjusted his sights. The Westland swung across the valleys and closed in for the kill. The Russians pounded up the ridge.

They went up the peak at a run, half crouched, and as they reached the top they burst out of the trees and into the light, as the fire burnt tenantless before them, and the Westland swooped out of the sky. They dropped flat and brought their rifles to their shoulders as Elliott's finger tightened on the trigger and Bede shot back the bolt. We heard those first shots, but there was no distinguishing which came from the air and which from the peak where the fire burned. It didn't matter. What did matter was that we had struck back. Weaponless, we had manoeuvred them into using their own strength on each other. It felt good. We began to walk faster.

Half an hour went by and then the Sikorsky flew past us, a mile away, straight past, not searching. Just going to pick up the wounded. There would be no search for us that night.

We marched until seven, when the day had faded completely, and headed down the north side of the range to find an obscure gully for the night. Our clothes were virtually dry by now, simply from the heat of our bodies, and when we lay down we felt we had done a good day's work. We felt drained and hungry and weak, but not beaten. Sam tore a young tree fern and handed round lumps of its pith. 'If we were able to roast it, it would taste very like dried apple,' he said. Unroasted, it tasted like old boots. We made a bed of ferns again, crept into them and slept.

The next morning was the worst so far, worse even than the day before, which was saying something. The cloud cover was just as thick as it had been the day before, and the inadequacy of all the rubbish we had been eating made itself felt. We were weak, pale and sick; I was feverish with cold, and Bill looked grey, drawn and sunken.

It took us longer than it should have done to stagger up to the ridgeback again, and when we got there it took longer than it should have done to work up to a decent speed.

An hour and a half after we started they returned. Together.

The Sikorsky was in the middle, flying low over the very centre of the range. There were two Westlands now, one on either side of the Russians. They too were flying low.

'They couldn't have joined forces, for Chrissake,' I said.

'They could have called a truce for the time being,' said Bill. 'Yesterday brought it home to them, must have. They've probably seen that if they don't co-operate we'll play one off against the other. Don't forget we represent a threat to both of them, if we get out, that is. The all-important thing is to catch us, whatever they do to settle it between them afterwards. It's a truce.'

'Time to get off this ridge, then,' said Sam. 'Sooner or later they're going to spot us. They'll just cruise up and down until they do. We're going to have to tackle a bit of difficult country.'

We waited till the choppers roared over us for the second time, and dropped off the ridge, diagonally down its flank. It was killer country.

The gully in which we had spent the night was exemplary. The whole side of the range consisted of gully after gully exactly the same, and there was nothing for it except to go up and down and up and down until it took as much willpower to put one foot in front of the other as it had when we had been stuck in the middle of the river two days ago. It was like hiking over a mountain of broken glass.

After an hour we rested for ten minutes, slumped against a tree trunk. As usual, Sam grubbed around and tried to find some item of vegetation he could claim was edible. He failed. He too dropped back against the tree trunk and closed his eyes. Tiny muscular spasms ran up and down his arms and legs and the sight was unnerving. Sam was the iron man of the party. If anybody could keep going, Sam could. I didn't meet Bill's eyes.

We rested too long and when the time came to move it was me who had to insist we did. Sam grinned wryly.

At last we came to a gully we could not climb out of: it was too steep and we were too exhausted. It wound straight down off the range in a roughly south-easterly direction and we followed it. Then it twisted back the wrong way, but by then we were too deep in it and there was nothing we could do. We plodded on down, waiting for a turning that never came. Far back up the mountainside we could hear the diminishing sound of the choppers, searching fruitlessly. There was no going back.

The gully came to an end about midday, in a well. That is the only way I can describe it: a well of mountains. We stood in a flat area, no larger than a football pitch, and the mountains rose up sheer all around us, black with bush, disappearing into the clouds. In the middle of the flat patch was a pool the same leaden colour as the sky. The stream from the gully flowed into it and nothing flowed out.

Sam and Bill slumped down in the wet ferns around it and I searched for food. When I brought back a handful of roots and grubs they were too tired and dispirited even to make the usual jokes. We simply ate and stared at the silent surface of the pool.

'We can't stay here,' I said. Nobody responded. 'Come on, you bastards. There's got to be a way out of here and we've got to find it. No use hanging around, is there?'

They both looked at me dully, and then forced strength into themselves. 'You're absolutely right, old son,' said Bill. 'Come on, Sam.'

We set off around the perimeter and after twenty minutes we found that there was no way out except the way we had come in. Apart from climbing.

'You've got to be joking,' said Sam.

We looked up at the black sheet of mountain and bush hanging in front of us, clouds clinging to it. I agreed with him.

'Look,' said Bill. 'We can't stop here because if they do come looking for us that'll be it. We can't get back the way we came. We've no bloody option. We have to go this way. You may have to give me a piggyback half-way up, but I'm going to give it a try.' And he began to scramble awkwardly up the creepers at the foot of the mountain, like an ant at the bottom of a skyscraper.

Sam and I began to follow. He was right; there was nothing else to do.

The climb took almost all the rest of the day. It was absolute hell for the first half-hour and worse afterwards. If it had been a rock face we would have recognized it as beyond our competence and strength and left it alone. But because it was covered in forest we thought we could make it, and we did. To rest we had to wedge ourselves against the trees. To climb we had to haul ourselves, faces pressed to the earth, from one piece of vegetation to another. Half-way up we climbed right through a belt of cloud.

By the last hour we had almost forgotten what we were there for. There were no helicopters to remind us that people were searching for us. There was no view through the trees of the drop below us. There was no indication of where the top of the mountain lay or how far ahead. All we were doing was inching upwards, endlessly and pointlessly. For all we knew it might have gone on for ever.

We reached the top about four-thirty in a sudden downpour of rain, and we stood there, knowing only that we did not have to climb any more, and seeing nothing. The rain poured through the trees and soaked us and none of us had the energy to go and look for shelter. We just propped ourselves against tree trunks and waited for it to stop.

By the time it stopped the day was beginning to die, but we saw three things, and not all of them were bad. We saw the range we had been forced to leave that morning snaking away miles to the south of us. We saw the three helicopters, tiny coloured dots in the distance, swooping and diving along its flanks, still looking for us. And we saw, or thought we saw, that the time had come to stop going south-east; that the long slope down from our peak took us eastwards, and that our best plan would be to go with it.

We were lucky to have discovered all these, luckier than we had any right to expect. And when, a few minutes later, all three choppers pulled up into the air and sped away for re-fuelling we felt a flicker of satisfaction. Not much, but a flicker. It led us astray.

'Do we rest for the night here?' asked Sam.

There was silence for a moment and then Bill spoke up. 'I don't think we should,' he said. 'The longer we spend here the weaker we get. The weaker we get the less chance we have of getting out. I think we should get as far as we can tonight. While we haven't got company.'

'I agree,' I said. 'It's downhill for a while anyway.'

'Right,' said Sam. 'We're off.'

It was a mistake that nearly cost us everything.

If you are tired and not much in control of your limbs, a long downward slope in the bush can be as wearing and bruising as a long climb. Gravity gets you moving and you bounce down from one irregularity of terrain to another, your arms catching at tree trunks to slow you, every step jolting the frame of your body until you feel it is going to fall apart. The long descent from the peak was like that, and as we went down light leaked from the sky and the forest filled up with the sort of darkness you only get after a dark day, and deep within me I felt that we were descending into a night from which we might never emerge. Quite apart from hunger and exhaustion and wet clothes, I was filthy – we all were – and few things are more demoralizing than dirt. Nobody said very much.

By seven o'clock it was pitch black and we had to strike a match to read the compass. The slope grew gentler, the ground more even, and we found ourselves in a broad shallow valley with a broad shallow river running through it. We waded into the river without much thought and half-way across disaster struck.

Sam heard it first, above the noise of the water, and stopped us. We stood stock-still, the river flowing past our calves, and listened. Nothing.

'Wait,' Sam said. Then we all heard it, and at the same time as we recognized the sound we saw them, all three sets of lights sweeping along the valley towards the ridge they had left that afternoon.

It was dark, but not dark enough. We felt the way mice must feel in an empty farmyard when the owl arrives. Suddenly the shadows look a long way away.

'Run for it,' hissed Sam. We splashed for the shore through the shallow current, and as we did someone up there with night glasses must have seen us, because two searchlights went on before we had made a dozen feet. We heard the sound of their engines rise to a higher pitch. The searchlights began to cut through the darkness like scythes. We put our heads down and ran.

Running through water is not easy. You can do it, if it's shallow enough, but it is effortful and slow. Running through that river while the choppers bore down on us was like hurdling through treacle. As we neared the bank and the water grew more shallow, our spray flew up around us like a wall. We seemed to be carrying it. If the river had had a shingle bank we would have been done for. If the forest had ended only a few yards farther from the water we would not have had time to cross the gap. If there had been ten yards more space between the forest and the river they would have landed their hunters there and then and they would have taken us within the hour.

None of these things were the case. There were no more than ten eternal seconds between splashing out of the current and hurling ourselves into the welcoming blackness of the bush, and then the scythes stopped and we could hear the helicopters circling, looking for somewhere they could come down, and while they circled we ran.

We never stopped running. I don't think I will ever stop running through that night. If the *Reader's Digest* demanded 'My Most Unforgettable Experience', that would be it.

They gave up trying to get their goons on the ground with us because they knew they would lose us if they wasted time looking for somewhere to drop them. They took off up the slope and for the next two hours their searchlights sliced the darkness of the forest like a master chef slicing meat while we ran between the lines of light, silent, unthinking, like animals. They had us on the run and we ran. If you ever want to invite me to a hunt, don't. I know how the fox feels.

The slope was as long and gentle as the one we had

descended and it wasn't murderous except in aggregate. When we reached the top we would have stopped and rested, but when we got there the trees were thin and the searchlights came right down between them and there was nowhere to stand and nothing to do except go on. We went down the other side and the other side was more like it, more like what we had grown used to, just as vicious as our stretched bodies had grown to expect. We bounced down it like rocks in an avalanche and there was a stream at the bottom and we collapsed at it and drank and drank and part of the reason we drank was just to experience some intense physical sensation apart from staggering through that black and hellish forest.

The beams of the searchlights swept up and down the creek and as they neared us we got to our knees and then our feet and started the climb out of the valley. It was the upward equivalent of the climb in.

By the time we got near the top the water we had swallowed was sweated out of us, cooling in the night air beneath our clothes. And when we reached the top we went down again.

It was like some fiendish roller-coaster ride. There was no end to it. Up one hog's-back; down into the valley; up the next hog's-back; on and on and on. It didn't stop us going eastwards, though. I think it was only that which kept us going. If we had been going in any other direction, if we had been realizing part of some complex and subtle strategy, we would not have been able to harness our bodies to our wills as we did. The nerves would have snapped, the muscles would have crumpled, we would have dropped into the damp earth until they found us.

But we were going east. We were heading straight for some internal vision of safety and help, and no one was going to stop us. Every ridge we climbed and crossed was another barrier behind us, another obstacle removed between hell and heaven, and as many obstacles as they put up, we would cross them, and that was that.

Bill was magnificent. A middle-aged man carrying the weight he had been carrying four days before could not have managed it. A middle-aged man who had eaten no proper food for two days should not have been able to manage it. But he managed it. He plodded along, and his breathing still sounded like a scrapyard in the middle of a revolution and the lines of exhaustion in his face looked as though they were being carved with chisels, but he never stopped. All the willpower that, throughout his life, he had put into making his mind work for him, he now put into making his body do the same, and the experiment worked. Sam was silent, uncomplaining, grim. Every now and then I tried to get out a cheerful remark. Each time it sounded like a Christmas carol in a graveyard.

We kept losing them and they kept finding us. A spot would pick us up for a second, through the canopy, and the choppers would bunch together, and we would zizag off in another direction, and twenty minutes later a wide sweep would catch us and they would be on to us again. But suddenly they had us, and had us good, because the fold of slope in which we were running left no chance to change course, and the spot picked us up half a dozen times in as many minutes. Like nails being hammered in.

Now the spot didn't lose us. It just rose in the air, straight upwards, and as it went the other two choppers went with it, and the night swallowed up their lights. We looked at each other.

'They have to refuel, the bastards!' said Sam. 'Thank Christ for that.' And we slowed. It took us twice as long to get to the top of the rise as it had to get half-way up. The pressure was off.

When we got to the top we stopped and the earth swung about us like a weight on the end of a pendulum. That passed, and we gazed into the darkness ahead and nobody asked how far there was to go because nobody had the answer. The compass told us what direction we had to follow and we followed it.

Before we left that place I looked behind, down from where we had come. There were torches in the forest. Fast torches. Torches moving faster than we were.

The choppers had left a present behind them. We tried to run.

The terror of the chopper pursuit had been real enough, but it was nothing compared to the fear that ate us now. The helicopters represented power and sudden death. The men who came after us now meant fury and hatred. I saw Karyanin's face again, as it screamed, and I knew he would be with them, however much he had been hurt, and that when he caught us he would exact retribution, and I feared him.

At the same time as the fear grew, strength ebbed. That strength could not have been very great to start with, for any of us, but within half an hour of that last blow being struck, we began to veer from side to side in our path and Bill began to stumble, and Sam and I supported him on either side, and before long we too were stumbling, falling, picking ourselves up again, and at last we fell and had no power to raise ourselves again. Across the other side of whatever anonymous valley we lay in, the torches descended through the trees, steadily, implacably, and fast.

We lay there among the creepers and waited for them to come and get us.

Bill had his eyes closed and I remember shifting my gaze from the moving lights to his face and contemplating it unthinkingly, while Sam's fingers dug into the earth again and again and the muscles of his arms and legs danced like wild things. We did not think of what we had hoped to gain, of what we would lose, of what we would come to, we were past all that. We just lay there like logs. Bill's eyes stayed closed for a long time, and I thought they would never open, but they did. They opened immensely slowly, like one of those slow-motion movies of an earthquake, where the ground parts before you. His pupils did not focus on me, or on the lights across the valley. They focused on a spot about a foot away. And as they focused they grew larger.

He levered himself up immensely slowly, with great effort, and leant forward into the blackness. When he sat back, he held in his hand a handful of tiny leaves. He brought them close to his eyes, ran his finger along their edges, and sniffed them.

I heard him say quietly to himself, 'Well, I'm blowed. These blighters.'

And then he leant forward and took a handful, and turned to us, and said: 'No questions, old sons. I'm not at liberty to answer them. But we've had a stroke of luck. Chew on these. Chew them slowly, and try and swallow them one at a time. Don't worry about the effects: they'll pass off.' And he handed each of us half a dozen of the leaves.

They tasted bitter, little different from any one of the bits of vegetation we had chewed on over the last few days. Before I had swallowed the first one, Bill was urging me to my feet.

'We'll try running, shall we? he said. 'May as well, I think we'll be able to keep it up for a little.'

I gave him a wry grin and got up and my muscles creaked like old leather. The torches were at the bottom of the valley now; they must have been crossing the stream. Minutes away.

We began to run downhill, clumsy and slow. Even this we could not hope to maintain. As we ran I swallowed the chewed leaves, one by one.

Half-way down the hill I was a foot taller – maybe seven feet. In the next dozen yards, for every inch I ran I gained an inch in height. The canopy of trees brushed against my cheek-bones; every stride was a good ten feet long. Beside me, Sam and Bill snaked into the air like wayward plants, rippling and curving like columns of smoke. An Arctic cold clasped itself about me and then fell away as the sun flowed from my belly outwards. My heartbeat began to pound in my ear as though stereo headphones had been clamped to my head. Between the beats voices came and went, spiralling into infinity, the voices of people leaning over the crib, over the sickbed, the voices of lovers and the voices of enemies. Beneath the voices was a steady primeval gibbering. There was too, for no reason, the distant noise of horsemen, the chink of metal on metal, the creaking of leather, and the beat of hooves far off, immensely far away, across the snow.

Every step took less effort, every stride grew longer than the last, and when we hauled ourselves up the slopes by the trees, we were catapulted and the ground fled behind us like water. The secret odours of every plant hung in the air like banners, and we saluted them as we passed.

Hammersham perched himself on my shoulder, blowing his cigar smoke into the night, telling me how he had loathed his father and how every edition of every paper he owned was piled like a stone on the old man's grave, to keep him there. I passed through the garden of statues on that island in the China Sea, each with its pair of sunglasses and its knife, and Murdoch ran from one to the other with a paintbrush, brightening the colours as they faded in the night-light.

I passed the tree-tops then and the clouds wreathed themselves around my face, and I passed through them too and the valleys and ridges were spread out beneath me like a crumpled eiderdown and the stars sang into my ears.

All the river of images that had flowed into me since childhood flowed out again, as though a dam had been burst, and music and dance and courage and beauty and terror gathered in a sea around me in technicolour tidal waves, whirlpools of grooved black plastic, an unwinding spool of pictures, unreeled across the ocean by the currents, looped and twisted down into the depths where the great creatures lie in the canyons of time.

I think it was midnight when the wind came, and the clouds began to part, and far, far away the little band of torches stopped and twisted themselves into a wild dance, and the wind tore the cover of clouds in two, and ran with us, ripping the clouds into tatters behind us, and together we went up the ridges and down the ridges and through the valleys and up the mountains and behind us the trees shrugged and rippled into vapour, and the wind took the vapour and blew it and we ran.

As dawn came the stars faded and I looked into the heart of the sun and saw it glowing and watched the earth turn and turn towards it, the oceans sliding like jelly and the towers leaning over as the planet moved. The sun glowed red and yellow and white and suddenly, in all its immemorial glory, it rose above the hill-tops and fused the sky, white, and then blue, and as it rose the heat ran slowly out of our limbs, and they shrank gently, gently, gradually telescoping, and down, down we went, through the canopy of leaves and into the forest, and the people who had come to see us waved respectfully and backed off and the heartbeats faded and the trees ceased to ripple and Sam and Bill formed and reformed themselves and with each metamorphosis they were smaller and the trees were higher above us.

There was no real sensation for a long time, no sense of being in the real world, just the great leaping movement of our bodies, and the forest around us coming and going as sound does on the edge of sleep. But slowly the times when everything was near became longer and the times when everything was distant became shorter and as the sun rose the drug drained out of us and we were going downhill and to move we had to make an effort and making efforts cost us strength we hadn't got, had never had, and the day came upon us.

Sam turned to us and said: 'I think we're going to make it, brothers. I think we're near the end. See that? That's the beginning of it.'

We looked across the valley at the slope ahead of us, and the slope was full of grey skeletons. The skeletons of trees.

The bush had grown again, twisting around them, clothing them; but fifty years of effort could not hide them. It looked like a battlefield where they had never cleared away the bodies.

'Nineteen twenties, I'd say,' said Sam. 'That was as far as they got, thank Christ. Probably the remains of a logging camp over the top of the ridge. It can't be a hell of a long way before we hit some sheep country.'

Neither of us understood him. He was telling us there was a chance, and both of us were too far gone to take it in. We just stared at the battlefield across the valley and stumbled down the slope towards it.

The stream was about four inches deep, eighteen inches wide, and we stood in front of it and didn't move. We were at the bottom of the valley and we weren't going to make it out of there. We just stood there, rocking gently on our feet. It felt as though all the hallucinated size and strength of the night march was collapsing in on us, tearing through the rotten fabric of our bodies, leaving tattered rags fluttering beside the stream. But don't include Sam in the diagnosis. The division of labour is one of the underlying principles of social existence, and during that trip it operated chronologically instead of laterally, so that as one of us began to go down under that intolerable pressure, another found the strength to support him, and it was as though we passed a torch between us, like runners in a relay race.

Now it was Sam's turn once more.

'Look, you bastards, listen to me,' he said, sticking his big face close to ours while we listened uncomplainingly. 'We are near the edge of the bush. We have a chance of getting help before they catch us. Don't just stand there, come on, start walking. Look, you only need to walk, just do it, just . . . Oh Christ. Have you forgotten about those blokes with the torches? They haven't just gone, you know, we haven't lost them; they can't be that far behind. They'll catch us up any time now.'

We stared at him intently, but his words blew away before they reached us.

'Come on, you bastards, walk, damn you, walk!' At last he took each of us by the arm and started to haul us along bodily, and we stumbled through the stream after him like zombies. When we got to the other side there was a path, going up the slope in great zigzags. All around it in the ferns lay ancient heaps of rubbish: rusted sawblades, tin cans, broken wood. All the time Sam dragged us he was cursing to himself. I watched the steam begin to rise gently from his shirt. I thought, 'The sun is with us again.'

Half-way up he stopped, and turned, and as I watched the expression on his face change I snapped out of it, and came to, and was in the world again. I turned round as well.

The Russians stood at the top of the slope we had just left. Two of them were kneeling down.

'Okay, this is it,' said Sam, and still grasping us he began to run, a painful, uneven run, but a run. I followed suit. Between us, still half asleep, Bill tottered along. We held him up; unnervingly light.

The bullets went wide, but the noise echoed around the valley like the cracks of doom. I didn't look round but I knew they had given up shooting at us from that far away and they were chasing us instead. Each section of the path stretched away ahead of us like a mile of motorway. My limbs were made of styrofoam. Bill's arm, held around my shoulder, felt like an old stick. His legs dragged. If we had had things together enough we would have asked ourselves just what was supposed to lie at the top of the path that was going to do us one jot of good against eight trained, armed and relentless men a few hundred yards behind us. If we had asked ourselves that question we would probably never have made it to the top. Each time we rounded a corner of the path and had another gradient to climb it was as though we had fallen to the bottom of that peak we had scaled the day before, and had to go up again.

By the time we had made the last one we could hear them grunting behind us. We stopped hearing that sound the second we came over the ridge-top. We stopped hearing anything and just looked.

Before us lay the world.

16 The Sawmill

The mountains had ended, that was the first thing. From the ridge where we stood they threw themselves lazily down in great crumpled slopes that turned into foothill, and far below the foothills became grazing country, stretching out in a haze of golden tussock to an unseen coast.

The sun shone down on it all from a huge, perfect sky, flawlessly blue, the air washed and clean after days of rain.

Immediately beneath us lay the amphitheatre.

It was a natural amphitheatre, a great bowl held in two of the descending arms of the mountains, and in the days of its prime it must have been filled with trees to match the Californian redwoods. Now it was scoured, stump-full, silent and empty, waiting for the play to begin.

At the far end, where the rim of the bowl fell away into a distant chasm, stood the sawmill. It was a crude, windowless box, its wood leached grey, its iron roof and chimney-stack red with rust. As soon as we saw it, it drew us. There was no logic in it, no rational thought, we just had to reach it.

Sam pulled Bill round to him and shook him. 'Mate,' he said. 'Bill, old mate: see that mill down there? Start going for it, will you? We'll join you in a minute. Okay?'

Bill nodded and began to descend slowly into the amphitheatre. Sam said: 'Delaying tactic number four. We've got to get this log moving,' and he kicked it.

I hadn't even seen the log. It lay at our feet at the apex of the ridge; six feet long and more than a yard in diameter, trimmed ready for a journey it had never made. It had been there so long that the earth had grown around it, and white ropes of fungus held it down.

We put our shoulders against it and shoved. It was like trying to push over a pillar-box. 'Lever,' said Sam, and grabbed at
a piece of branch. I followed suit, thrusting the branch under
the log and leaning upwards. It was like trying to lever a pillar-
box. A light sweat of impatience broke over me as it had done
before Karyanin's body in that hotel room, and I felt the rain-
soft earth give beneath the lever. Move, damn you, move.

We could hear them now, really hear them. We couldn't see
them because of the bush, but at any minute they would burst
up the last section of the path and that would be that.

The lever dug into my collar bone and all the empty muscles
of my arms said: 'Sorry, brother, can't be done,' but I kept on
shoving.

Suddenly the log moved. The ropes of fungus broke and it
rocked in its bed of earth. It teetered on the edge of the drop
and then rolled back. The first of them rounded the corner
then. It was Karyanin, of course.

I threw my entire weight into the lever in a reflex paroxysm
of terror. I heard Sam grunt and it gave; it went over the edge
and thundered down the path at them. We turned and leapt
away then, in a great surge of elation, springing down the slope
and into the bowl with strength we had not had for days.

Before we were half-way across, the Sikorsky appeared from
the south, and high in the sky above it were the bright dots of
the Westlands. Their shadows raced towards us over a sunlit
earth, and suddenly the amphitheatre changed. There would be
no play, no chorus, but another sort of spectacle, and all
around the silent banks the sated spectators beat their knees
and roared for blood.

The earth around us began to explode in little puffs of dust
as they came in for the kill.

Bill reached the sawmill then and threw himself at the great
grey door. It swung inwards with a high shriek from its rusted
hinges, and he disappeared into its darkness.

Sam gave a gasp, a sort of high, surprised cry, reeled sideways and smashed into the ground. I didn't stop to pick him up.
I was behind him and as he went down I caught up with him

and grabbed him under both arms and just kept going, half dragging him, while the blood oozed out over my fingers and the amphitheatre filled with the clamour of the choppers the way a tin bucket fills with water.

Then Bill came lumbering out of the mill, yelling at the top of his voice, I don't know what, and we were both staggering along with Sam between us. Before the first chopper touched down we were over the threshold of the mill and we laid Sam down in the darkness. The door swung back behind us and as it closed I saw the Sikorsky settling on to the ground and the two Westland Gazelles coming down beside it. The door crashed into place and the light went.

'There's no bolt,' said Bill.

'The logs,' said Sam, from the ground. 'That pile of crap there, beside the door, knock it over, tip it against the door. Quick!'

His eyes had got accustomed to the darkness more swiftly than ours and he lay there, the blood oozing from his shoulder, directing us. I blundered into the heap of half-cut timber and began to tear at it blindly, hauling the beams out and hurling them at the door. The splinters sank into my flesh and the rats scuttled away from me, farther into the mill. Suddenly I pulled out the key timber and as the first shoulder hit the door the whole pile collapsed, and it was blocked, the entrance was no longer an entrance, and we were shut in. Silence fell.

Bill knelt beside Sam, tore a strip from his shirt, and wiped away the blood. 'Very lucky,' he said. 'Went straight through. Wait till I bandage it.' I tore one of the sleeves off my shirt for the bandage, and then tied the other to one of Bill's for a sling. We eased Sam into a sitting position.

They fired three shots into the walls then, and Murdoch's voice, through a loudhailer, shouted something.

We couldn't make out what he was saying. None of the bullets came through into the mill. That meant something. Something important. It meant the walls were made of very thick timber. And there were no windows and no more doors. They were outside and we were inside. They couldn't get in and we couldn't get out. Stalemate.

Exhaustion should have seized me then, because I had gone through every reserve of strength I'd ever had, but it didn't because of the adrenalin. I must have had about as much adrenalin careering round my system as you usually get to use in five years. I began to roam around in the cobwebbed darkness.

I am always fascinated by the way things gradually become visible in a darkened room: the way beams of light suddenly appear in pitch blackness. They are there all the time, of course, but you can't see them. Gradually they grow in brightness and intensity, and the darkness around them fades to a sort of grey. You wonder how it was you couldn't see them before.

The beams of light getting into the mill came through half a dozen tiny holes in the corrugated iron roof. Gradually I began to use them.

The place was a fantastic mess. Too fantastic to be simply the debris left when an operation closed down in the normal course of things. Some disaster must have struck, perhaps a bankruptcy, perhaps an epidemic; perhaps a distant war had called the men to go and sink their axe-blades into other men, instead of into the flesh of trees.

Whatever the cause, the mill was solid with junk. Most of it was wood; rough-cut trunks and logs, great slices of tree-smashed branches, chips and heaps of sawdust with a faint resined pungency after all these years. Beneath the wood lay the equipment they had left and that seemed to be most of it – blocks and tackle, two-man saws, sledge-hammers and mallets. In the middle of the mill were two huge saw-tables with a slit in the centre of each, and from one of them the black, rusted disc of the sawblade still reared up towards the roof. To the left of the tables were the saw-pits, dark water glistening with slick at the bottom. On the other side of the mill was the steam engine.

Even in ruins it was a thing of beauty, like something from a Victorian fairground, seething with trimmings and little plaques bearing the names of the firm which had made it in some Glasgow factory endless years ago, before so many things had come upon the world. One of the shafts of sunlight from the roof lit a patch of untarnished brasswork and the whole machine seemed to gleam, ready to spring back into life again as if the second half of the twentieth century had never happened. I ran my hand over the grimy surface of its boiler, and felt the interlocking cogs of its gear wheels. I let myself imagine the smell of the woodsmoke as they thrust the timber waste into its glowing heart, and the gear wheels began to turn and the sawblades began to scream as the logs slid towards them over the table. Then I walked back to where Bill sat with Sam.

Everything was quite still, quite silent. I slid down into the sawdust beside them and we looked at each other. Nobody said anything, because it had all been said. We had run the gamut of the emotions of hope and despair and terror and now we were simply sitting here, drained of everything and ready to let whatever was going to happen, happen. We had gambled for everything and it had brought us here, into this rubbish tip on the edge of despair, and we had only to wait. I looked at Sam, at his face white with pain under the dirty growth of beard, at the bandage around his shoulder which was slowly staining itself with his blood. I looked at Bill and it was like looking at a mattress from which the stuffing has been torn, piece by piece. The folds of skin hung around his face like pieces of old, old cloth. His torn shirt hung buttonless over his belly and beneath it I could see the sweat-black band of the money belt. It didn't mean anything any more. We sat there like that for about ten minutes, and nothing happened. The rats moved about somewhere in the gloom, looking for new places to hide, but that was all.

At the end of ten minutes the hissing started. It is always a sinister sound, whether from a crowd or a machine, and in those circumstances we shrank from it in something like superstitious terror. It was coming from under the door. My first irrational conviction was that it was some animal they had, some living thing they were going to unleash on us. It was about ten seconds before we realized what it was. They were going to use gas.

It was a very neat solution. I didn't think that in those first seconds but I realized it quite soon. If they had set fire to the place, which must have been the other most attractive idea, they would have destroyed what they wanted above all to reclaim. If they had succeeded in smashing their way in they ran the same risk and they would probably have suffered casualties. But this way all they had to do was open the valves on a few cylinders, poke tubes into the knot-holes, and wait. People always ask during hostage sieges why the police don't use gas. The reason is that all the gases available to them take too much time: hostages can be killed in that time. But we had no hostages, nothing we could threaten them with, and there was absolutely nothing we could do to stop them. The gas filtered in, a hint of sulphur in its smell, flowing along the floor like ground mist. We got up and began to retreat before it into the mill. Big beads of sweat began pouring down Sam's face. He was struggling to control himself. He stumbled over a piece of rubbish and fell backwards. We hauled him to his feet again. He was shaking like a leaf. Bill and I looked at each other.

A second and a third cylinder were opened outside. The hissing was coming from three places now. The air was becoming thick.

Suddenly there was a thud on the roof, and an odd rolling sound, like a sail being unfurled. The light went. They'd thrown a tarpaulin over the roof, covering the holes. The mill was plunged into blackness. Bill began to cough.

'Got to get out,' said Sam, between his teeth. 'Got to get out of this goddam rat-hole,' and he tried to break away from us for the door. Bill grabbed him. 'You walk out of that door into a coffin,' he said. 'That's exactly what they want. They're waiting for us.'

'Well, what do we bloody do, then?' said Sam, and nobody replied.

I stared into the darkness and tried to let the thought formulate itself. I knew it was there, had been there for some minutes now, but I was too exhausted to bring it to a shape I could recognize. Then it was there, obvious, undeniable, and I knew what we had to do.

'They brought the logs in through the door we used,' I said. 'But they didn't take them out that way. They can't have done. There must have been some way out at the far end when they'd sawn them up. Mustn't there?'

We turned and peered into the pitch-black mill, beyond the saw-tables. The far wall was a solid heap of broken timber, six feet deep. If there was anything behind it we would have to shift every log. Silence. We let that sink in. Then Bill said: 'It's worth a try. Sam, stay here, bang about with this bit of wood and shout out to them. Doesn't matter what you shout. It'll just keep them occupied while we try shifting the stuff at the end. Will you do that?'

'Okay,' said Sam. 'But get a move on.'

We scrambled over the debris until we were jammed between the saw-tables and the logs. Bill said quietly: 'It was a good thought, it'll keep Sam occupied, but I don't think there's much chance. When you were looking at this place from the ridge-top, did you see it was on the edge of a drop? There's a cliff on the other side of this wall, old son!'

'It's worth a try,' I said. 'Anything's worth a try. Let's get going.'

We did the job almost silently, but at a cost in speed. Bill supported the pile while I pulled out the logs and laid them behind us on the saw-table. The normal order of events was reversed. Instead of getting progressively less able to continue as the heap went down our strength grew, and with it, our speed. All the time Sam yelled and banged incoherently at the other end of the mill. By the time the gas forced him back towards us we were going at that black heap like crazed creatures, silent and desperate. The hissing never stopped. It was too dark to see the gas any more, but the air was thick with sulphur and with every breath more of it seeped down into our lungs. It seemed to fill the spaces inside my face and throat, burning them like acid, and gradually, even as the pile behind us grew and the pile before us diminished, I could feel it tugging at my brain, unravelling it gently, pulling it to pieces. I tore at the logs, digging my fingers into the wood as a hold on reality. It was getting hard to see, and it wasn't just the light. Bill and Sam faded and faded again, and I could feel myself going.

Log after log came away and the wall began to appear.

The wall. Not a door, just a wall. Just the same thick grey planks that surrounded us everywhere else. I'd been wrong. There was no way out. The mill was filled to the brim and there was nothing we could do except breathe it in deep and die in the darkness. I heard Sam grinding his teeth, forcing himself to stay quiet. I felt panic rising in me like vomit. Then the wall moved.

I could just make out Bill's shape, leaning against it a few feet away. 'Shove to your left, old son,' he whispered, and I did, and the wall moved again. 'Panel,' Bill breathed. 'Runner rusted. Sam, chuck something at the far end, couple of things, drown the noise.'

Bill and I took a deep breath of the darkness and the poison and thrust at the panel. Rust flaked down on us like rain and the screech of metal on metal bit into our ears. It didn't matter. The panel slid back, and light and air flooded into the mill.

We stood there and whooped it in and in front of us the whole panorama shifted and settled as the oxygen filtered back into our bloodstreams and the poison filtered out. It was the same view we had seen from the top of the ridge, the same sweep of foothill and second-growth bush, the same expanse of golden hills and plain in the distance. The only additional feature was the chasm, a hundred feet deep, two hundred yards wide, yawning beneath our feet, and filled with unreachable and untouched bush. The timbermen must have cut their way through the forest up from the plains, and seen, like some green Eldorado on the other side of the gap, the rich stands of timber in the amphitheatre. Greed had stirred them then, stirred them to a feat of bush engineering that was amazing even now, fifty or more years later.

They had thrown a great, crude trestle structure across the

gap, huge trees lashed and pegged and clamped together, and across the trestles ran the tracks for a bush railway. The tracks ran out of the bush on the other side, across the trestles, and straight into the sawmill, straight into the debris where we stood.

Bush railways cropped up all over New Zealand in the heyday of native bush forestry in the nineteenth and early twentieth centuries, stretches of a mile or two of tram track with a team of horses or a steam winch as the motive power, and bogeys on to which the rough-cut or dressed logs were roped for the journey to a road-head. Most of them have disappeared long ago, the rails pulled up for scrap, the sleepers rotted into the humid floor of the bush, quite forgotten.

The railway in front of us was not in this category. The rails were red with rust, the sleepers and the trestles looked like old bones, but it seemed to be intact. There were no gaps in the two hundred yards between where we stood and the other side of the chasm. I suspect that even if there had been it would not have stopped us.

We did not pause to think about it for a moment. We were beyond that.

'Where's the bogey?' said Sam. 'They must have left the bogey,' and we threw ourselves once more at the heaps of rubbish. The tracks ran right through a pile of sawdust and under the saw-table. I reached into its darkness and felt around. There was cold metal under my hand. I took it, and pulled, and the bogey ran out, bumped over the sawdust and stopped at our feet.

It consisted simply of four wheels, a metal frame, and four broad planks fitted into the frame. There should have been a fifth, but there wasn't. 'What about the cable?' whispered Bill.

I crawled over the saw-table and found the drum, next to the steam engine. All the cable was there, but it would never support anything again. It was rusted solid. I went back to the others. 'If we go down on that thing, there'll be no changing our minds half-way.'

'Who wants to change their mind?' Sam said, and grinned and climbed aboard. Bill joined him, gripping tight on to the metal frame. I stood for a moment, looking out at the great sunlit scene outside, and at the ancient bridge we were trusting our lives to. Then I half lay, half knelt on the bogey, and kicked us off.

For the first few feet of track inside the mill it was all a matter of kicking and shoving while the rust broke around the axle and the bogey creaked painfully along, but as we emerged from the darkness of the mill and into the dazzling sunshine all that changed. It changed because of something we hadn't noticed. The incline. The bridge sloped up to the sawmill. The track sloped down across the chasm. It made for speed. The bogey began to travel as if it had been catapulted. It was terrifying.

The fifth plank was the worst aspect. The plank that wasn't there. There was no way short of closing your eyes to stop yourself looking straight down through the bogey, through the sleepers, and down into the chasm. It was like looking over the edge of the world. Half-way across the whole structure shifted under our weight, shuddering like some dying beast. My stomach shrank once more to golf-ball size. Down below, the forest slid away like water.

I concentrated. I concentrated on something else. I concentrated on the faces of the men in front of the sawmill, smiling while the cylinders emptied and the banging from the interior died away, and waiting, waiting those extra minutes until we were quite finished, before they cut their way in.

And then their faces changed. They listened. And they began to run for the choppers. If you measure time in terms of fear it took about an hour to cross the chasm, but I suppose if you were looking at a stopwatch it would hardly have registered. The drop rocketed away behind us and we were on the other side and into the bush. None of us had considered what would happen when we got there; none of us could have conceived what did.

Freed of the constraints of the bridge, the builders had simply tipped their railway straight down the mountainside. And the bogey went with it.

If we had been terrified when we shot out over the bridge, we were now something else, but I don't know the word to convey it. There is something peculiarly horrifying about totally unrestricted speed and when you have no control whatever over the vehicle you are riding, the horror is squared.

The bush began to stream past us as if it was being squirted out of high-pressure hose. Inches below our faces the forest floor was one long blur. I gripped the frame of the bogey until blood ran out from under my nails. Beneath me Sam and Bill were rigid with fear. It was incredible.

I only registered the screaming from the track then, which is an indication of how preoccupied I had been with the other sensations because the noise the wheels made on the tracks was like more banshees than you ever heard. Sparks flew as if there was someone with an arc welder down there. As a mobile firework display we would have won any competition in the world. We just went.

When the helicopters did arrive we never heard them; just the bullets: a crash like a window breaking and then a long evil whining journey into the bush when they ricocheted off. If the people firing them had been able to see us, they would have killed us.

As it was they just made it feel as though we were going down a roller-coaster through a meat grinder. I wanted my money back.

About fifty seconds after they caught up with us the track began to curve, and if there is one thing more terrifying than going straight down a gradient like that on a winchless bogey it is going down such a curved gradient. At no point did any of the four wheels actually leave the track and rear up in the air the way cars do in movies when they go round a corner, but they came so close to it that it didn't matter. In addition there is the human problem of not being able to see around corners. You can't see the place where the salvage men have started ripping up the track, or the point where the track-layers got tired of building it, or the point where a large and immovable tree has fallen across your prescribed route.

You can just close your eyes and yell soundlessly into the wind and watch the bullets bouncing off rails in front of you.

You ask me how long that went on for and I can't tell you that either, because it just felt like the seven ages of man rolled into one. All I can tell you is that in the end the track straightened enough and the trees thinned enough for me to be able to see what did lie ahead. And to wish I couldn't.

It was the end of the bush. It was still a long way away, miles away and far below, but we could see it: the line where the dark green of the forest ended and the golden, heat-hazed sheep grazing country began. There were roads down there and far away, really far, what might have been the flash of sunlight on a windscreen or a farmstead window.

But before we got there lay the river. The river in the gorge. It was the last straw.

It was different from the chasm. It was no deeper, probably, possibly a little narrower. But in the blow to the stomach stakes there was no competition. For two reasons.

The first reason was we could not see the bridge. There might have been a bridge, there might not. For all we knew the track would take us straight to the edge and we'd sail off, past a little notice saying, 'The East Coast Demolition Company has removed the bridge as a risk to life on the order of the Rural District Council.'

The second reason was that we were going at what felt like about a hundred miles an hour, and even if there was a bridge the chances of staying on its rails at that speed would have made those of a snowball in hell look like an insurance policy.

The bogey went for the river as if it had been born there. We went with it. We had no option. We were bound to follow that track until it tired of us. We were secured to it. And if the killers above turned us into dead meat on that bogey, well, that was the way it was meant to be.

There was still no sign of a bridge.

They never stopped firing once. They never hit us once either. Until they saw the bridge. That stopped them. They weren't fools.

They must have seen the bridge at the same time as we did and all concerned realized immediately that though there was a bridge there was no need for any more bullets. There is no point in hurling bullet-riddled bodies into a public river if you can achieve the same effect by letting the people you don't like just smash themselves to pieces on the way down. That was how they reasoned, I know it.

That was how I reasoned too.

The bridge looked like the Bridge on the River Kwai during those moments in time when it was being blown up. It was built on the same principle as the bridge before the sawmill. The only difference was that about a third of the timbers were missing. And it was clear where they had gone: the river had taken them. It foamed and spat around the remaining trestles. Waiting for us.

The entire bridge was slumped towards the opposite bank, like a pack of cards going over. If we had not been able to observe it for several consecutive seconds we would have sworn it was in movement. But if it was not in movement now, there was no question that it would be in about twenty seconds from now, when the bogey hit it.

When I am an old, old man, ask me about those twenty seconds and they will still exist for me with all the acid vividness that they did then. As each one of them passed, more and more of the earth leaked away into another dimension.

It was a relief to hit the bridge: it was a relief to get it over with and know that all we had to do was die. As soon as the bogey hit those stretched and tortured rails the bridge began to go.

We went with it.

The odd thing was the silence. It must have been some freak of hearing rather than of reality, but the moment the bogey reached the bridge there was no sound at all: no screeching from the wheels, no roar from the helicopters; and down below, in the gorge, the river seething silently, lifting boulders and smashing them silently against the walls of the gorge.

The bridge was collapsing, folding up on itself like a concertina, falling steadily from one side of the river to the other, and we went with it.

It was falling the same way that we were going. The rails were tilting themselves eastwards with us, and as they tilted the bogey slid down them, slid straight down at the opposite side. For a fraction of a horrifying second we were high above the other bank, and then the whole thing slumped and the bogey shot down the buckling rails and off into the bush, while behind it the bridge slithered into the river and the remnants of the track trailed down after it like a tail.

It didn't matter to us at all. To me nothing mattered. As I went off the bogey and the bogey hurled itself at the trees, a branch struck me across the forehead, leaving a mark I bear to this day, and the world went black.

Bill pulled me up, Bill and Sam together, and we started running through the trees, just running, and the storm of bullets started again the second we did.

We ran on to the road where the road ended, and it was a little while before we recognized it as a road. We'd got out of the habit of such things.

To be fair, as a road, it didn't rank highly. It was no more than a bulldozed strip through the forest with broken trees and piles of glistening yellow clay on either side. The only factor that made it a road above all roads was the Land-Rover, straining towards us round the last bend. Full of amazed people.

It wasn't until we saw the expressions on their faces that it came home to us just what a state we were in. But if I had seen three such ragged, bearded, blood-stained, filthy, gesticulating creatures come hobbling out of the trees, I too would have been amazed. Ben Gunn had nothing on us. But it didn't stop them pulling the Land-Rover to a halt and jumping out.

'Get back in again, get back in the bloody car again, quick!' I shouted at them. The blood was pouring down my forehead from the fight with the branch. I remember tasting it when I opened my mouth. As I spoke I shoved Sam towards the open door.

Three of them had got out, three big blokes dressed for the bush and hunting. Two of them looked like brothers and they had red beards. They didn't try to stop Sam from getting into the Land-Rover.

'What the hell is going on, mate?' said the older of them. 'Who are you?'

'Our friend has been shot,' said Bill, between gasps for breath. 'There's helicopters after us, and we are all of us in considerable danger. Would you have the kindness to turn the car round and help us get him to a hospital as soon as possible?'

One of the red-bearded ones said: 'Look, mate, no offence and all that, but if you've had a shooting accident you've had a shooting accident. There's no need to say that blokes in helicopters are taking potshots at you, you know. Look here . . .'

He never finished the sentence. The Sikorsky shot out of the trees and began to descend immediately on to the road. Before any of us had finished getting back into the Land-Rover the first bullets were bouncing off the bonnet. 'Jesus Christ,' said the big man. 'My apologies, mate,' and he slammed the Land-Rover into reverse as the first bullet starred the windscreen.

We were on the last lap.

17   A Ride in a Land-Rover

One second's hesitation and it would have been a very short
lap indeed, because the Sikorsky was not the only helicopter
trying to land on the road. The other one was the green Westland, and it wanted to land behind us. If they had both achieved
their objective the Land-Rover would have been shut in like
an insect in a matchbox.

The Westland never had a chance.

The Land-Rover shot back down the track as though somebody big had kicked it, and as we went back the Westland
came down and I knew it was going to hit us and at the last
minute I closed my eyes and when I opened them again the
chopper's engine was screaming immediately overhead and we
were still going backwards at the same speed. What the guy in
the Westland felt like I didn't know and didn't care. I had other
things to worry about. We all had.

If ever a road was not designed for reversing down, it was
that road. To be perfectly frank I don't think it had been
designed very well for going up, either, but be that as it may.
Any road sign which had attempted to convey how many hair-
pin bends the road contained would have had to have been
about twelve feet square, because the road was nothing but
hairpins, and it went on for a long time. It seemed to go on for
ever.

There was nowhere to turn, you see: on one side there was
a six-foot clay bank and on the other side a long drop over a
crumbling clay edge into whatever was down there. And the
road wasn't wide enough anyway. All we could do was go
backwards as fast as possible, and the guy with the red beard
at the wheel, who turned out to be called Murray when we got

around to things like that, was twisted around from his smashed windscreen, looking behind, sweat pouring down his face and spreading in great arcs from his armpits. He kept up a constant stream of obscenities but he never took his foot off the accelerator. It was terrifying.

Of course it wasn't only the fear of going down a steep, winding, mud mountain road backwards and too fast: on its own that would have been nothing. What made it uncomfortable was the bullets and the helicopters. The helicopters came too close and the bullets came even closer. If it hadn't been for the trees both would have come closer still, but the trees were tall and their branches spread a long way and it gave us a fifty-fifty chance of getting round the next bend without being gunned down. We took it. We didn't have any option.

There was one other factor that made three of us more uncomfortable than the rest. That was the realization that we had made a serious mistake. That realization dawned on us when the first bullets bounced off the bonnet at the top of the track. What was that realization? It was that even though we had reached civilization, even though we had found a fairly hefty group of witnesses, neither of our opponents was going to give up.

If you remember rightly we had banked on this. We had told ourselves that while the bush was a good place to hide in, it was dangerous, because while in the bush neither the Russians nor the Americans were constrained by the laws of the land or the Geneva Convention. We took our chances about being found on the assumption that once we got out they wouldn't be able to touch us.

We had been wrong. We had underestimated how much both parties wanted what we had got. We had underestimated how mad they were. And we had to pay for that mistake.

With any other group of human beings the simple fact that powerful and determined people were trying to stop them would have been enough to do just that. With this group that was not the case. To that extent we were outrageously lucky.

The Land-Rover was packed – and when I say packed I

mean packed – with scions of the local farming community out for a few days' hunting. They were prepared for some hardship and excitement and if this was the way it was going to happen, this was the way it was going to happen. Also, early as it was, a number of them had been drinking. In fact most of them had been drinking. We gathered later that the festivities had begun the night before and the period of time between them ending and the hunting trip starting had been very brief indeed.

So instead of stopping the Land-Rover and piling out of it with their hands up, they smashed the windows through and poked their heads out and yelled rude things at the helicopters and banged on the roof with beer cans.

And all the time the Land-Rover kept going down backwards and round the hairpins at a sickening speed. Seven minutes away from the top of the track we went over the edge.

There was a lurch that was a lot more sickening than the trip backwards had been, a great thud as the chassis hit the road, and then we stopped. We threw ourselves out of the side that wasn't hanging over the drop, took a long shocked look at what had happened and began to scramble down the bank. We had forty seconds to get the Land-Rover back on to the road again before the massacre. We didn't know we had forty seconds at the time but we did. The reason was that helicopters which can travel at nearly two hundred miles an hour take a little while to stop and turn round when they have overshot whatever it is down in the forest below they are following. In the event that little while was forty seconds. As I say, we didn't know that at the time. All we knew was that our means of escape was immobilized, we were outside on the road instead of inside and if we didn't get a move on we would probably end up dead.

Down below in the green bush a little stream gurgled and sang, as little streams are wont to do, whatever the circumstances. The earth was raw and wet, full of broken trees smashed when they had made the road and we slithered about in it, trying to get a purchase, trying to find the right hold on the Land-Rover to heave it back on to the road.

It was a very long forty seconds. It was physically arduous and psychically no small strain. And by the time that goddam wheel was back on the road again, and the first helicopter was hovering above us like a wasp, and the Land-Rover was moving and we were jumping aboard as it went, something had united us, and we were a team.

During the second half of the trip down the mountainside, Bill gave a cool, brief and convincing account of what they needed to know. Those who were sober enough to be impressed were impressed. Those who weren't drank to us. At the wheel Murray's knuckles strained like huge white walnuts, and the sweat spread right over his back.

'Murray,' said a guy who was called Eric, 'if I remember rightly there's a place you can turn about three bends down. It's a blind track into the bush on one of these corners. You could back straight into it as you go round and shoot straight out again.'

'Good on you, mate,' said Murray. 'We'll try it.' At the back of the Land-Rover a bullet hit one of the piled-up packs, and something inside it burst loudly. The engine sounded like a soul in torment.

We got our reward just where Eric had said we would. Murray saw the exit as we came into the bend and he stepped on the gas and took his foot right off the clutch. The bush closed over us like the green waters of a pool.

Ten feet and the track ended and we stopped. Murray twisted round so that he was looking forwards, with a long sigh of relief, and then he said, half to himself: 'Right.' He slid the Rover into gear and hit the accelerator. We shot out of the bush and on to the road like a greyhound out of its trap. And we never stopped.

I should have been nervous going down a road like that at speeds like that and with friends like that hovering overhead. But I wasn't. I was elated. Consider soberly what has gone before and you may sympathize. There was another reason too. We were armed again.

Someone called Gary thought of it first: unwrapped his rifle,

loaded it, shoved it through one of the broken windows, and
fired it. I don't know if it hit anything but it sounded terrific.
Everybody wanted to try it. Everybody except us had a rifle.
The Land-Rover went round the first bend as though we were
on a straight stretch of the M1 and before it had completed its
turn it must have looked like a berserk porcupine. It fairly
bristled with rifle barrels. Inside it sounded like we were having
a rock-throwing party. It sounded like the clappers of hell. It
sounded terrific. Murray drove like a maniac, Bill talked like a
professor of genetic engineering, Sam and I broke open the
ammunition, and everybody else fired. It was terrific.

'Where's the nearest place we can get a plane?' asked Bill.

'Nearest airstrip's at Amber,' said Murray. 'Amber's twenty
miles from here. There's a strip there for top-dressing planes.'

'Any chance of getting a ride?'

'Could be,' said Murray. 'Mate of mine called Norm Bailey's
based there. He'd fly you out, I reckon. Problem'll be getting
there, won't it?'

'You're doing all right now,' I said.

'They can't land on the road now,' said Murray. 'Another
ten minutes and we'll hit open country and after that there's
the plains. There'll be nothing to stop them easing the throttle
forward and sitting on the road a quarter of a mile ahead of
us. There'd be no option then except to stop, would there?'

To which nobody replied.

The bush ended abruptly, as though sliced off with a knife,
and the sun hit us as it had never done since the day I left the
bus at Rotorua and climbed into the darkness of the pines. It
reflected off the vast expanse of dry golden tussock that lay
ahead as though it was a mirror. It was hot country, dry
country, and all the shadows were sharp. The heat rolled towards us and surged all around us like a freak tide.

Once upon a time it had all been covered in bush like the
rest, but the bush had been cut and burnt again, and grazed
and grazed again, and now it was grassland and the forest
could not reclaim it.

The foothills pierced the plains in long, broadly-rounded peninsulas with dry stream-beds in shallow valleys between them. The only trees were cabbage palms, leather-trunked, leather-leafed, isolated amid the grasslands. You could see them from miles away. The air smelled of baked hillside and warm grass. In the far distance there were the dark lines of shelter belts and long, undeviating roads, constantly shifting in the heat haze. It all looked as though it were blissfully sound asleep.

The road was metalled now; that is, the mud surface had been covered by pebbles scooped from some distant river-bed, to give it greater solidity in the winter. Two deep tyre-tracks ran straight down the centre of the road through the metal and the pebbles flew up against the bodywork as though they were trying to tell us something.

The choppers did just what Murray had said they would do. The moment the sunlight hit us they pulled high up into the perfect sky and rocketed ahead. We roared down the road after them. There was nowhere else to go.

Two minutes later the road swung round a gentle bluff, straightened, and went down at the plains in a long, gentle run. At the bottom of it was a cattle-grid. Fifty feet the other side of the cattle-grid sat the Sikorsky. Behind the Sikorsky sat the green Westland. In the air above them the red Westland hovered, waiting.

There was nothing we could do.

Everything was suddenly very quiet in the Land-Rover. Nobody was firing, nobody was talking, nobody was banging beer cans on the roof. Everybody was watching the roadblock. Through the heat haze we saw a line of men clamber out of the choppers and kneel down on the road. They were holding something to their shoulders. Sunlight glinted off the barrels.

Murray kept his foot down. We were eight hundred yards away from the cattle-grid. The eight hundred yards dwindled away to five hundred, to three hundred, to two hundred; he didn't shift his foot an inch and the yards disappeared as though somebody was swallowing them. We could see the whites of their eyes. We could see down the barrels of their goddam rifles.

You can't ram them, you bastard, you'll kill us all. Nobody said it. Everybody thought it. Get your bloody foot off that gas-pedal, Murray, for Chrissake! He never moved it an inch.

Ten feet from the cattle-grid he spun the wheel like rope through his hands and the Land-Rover suddenly and terrifyingly leapt out of the ruts and across the metalled road and into the fence.

Most fences in New Zealand are made of something known as number eight fencing wire, stretched between sturdy posts let into holes in the ground every few yards. Between the posts the wires are kept apart and the fence given solidity by wooden battens stapled to the wire. It's an effective and economical fencing system and hundreds of square miles of the country are divided up with it.

Murray hit the fence at a point midway between two of the sturdy posts. The battens smashed and the wires stretched around the bonnet of the Land-Rover like elastic. They snapped suddenly, the way elastic does, and then we were through.

As they snapped, Eric brought down the Westland. When I said everybody had been sitting there like a taxidermist's window display, I must exempt Eric. Eric trusted Murray. Eric was still largely sober. As we neared the roadblock, Eric had been lining up on the one helicopter that remained in the air. As Murray swung off the road, Eric fired.

As the wire snapped, the Westland blew up. It turned into a great, blood-red fireball and fell down on to the road like a dead bird. There were two more explosions as it hit the ground. It was as simple as that.

I don't know if there was any space between the accelerator and the floor when we went off the road, but if there wasn't, Murray must have jammed his foot right through when we hit the field. It was a big field, and it may have been full of interesting land formations, but I didn't see any of them. Thirty seconds after we entered the field we left it on the same basis.

The second fence gave and snapped like elastic and by the time we were through both helicopters were up in the air again and neither of them was spending any time looking for beauty spots.

Behind them the sky was filling with a big black plume of oily smoke. And then the sheep came charging towards us.

You're not impressed by a stampede of sheep? It doesn't sound like the most dangerous thing in the world and it probably isn't. There are probably few circumstances in which a stampede of sheep can be fatal. That was one of them. If we got caught up in that terrified mass of animal stupidity that would be that. We would have as much chance as a fly on a piece of fly-paper. Murray hauled the wheel round, the Land-Rover spun, and we accelerated across the field back the way we had come. The Sikorsky and the Westland overflew us midway.

We weren't going fast enough to break another hole in the fence, so Murray spun us round again and we roared away down the field with the sheep coming up on us in a bleating horde and the helicopters swinging back again in mid-field.

It was then that the farmer appeared. He was a short man, with a great barrel chest and fists like hams. He had a big, round, red face and grimy green sun-bonnet, such as toddlers used to wear, perched on top of his head. He was riding a Japanese motor-bike with big balloon tyres designed for riding up mountains. He was coming towards us fast, swinging his head from side to side, with his mouth open. When he came nearer I understood that he was saying, 'What the bloody hell?' over and over again, like a litany.

'Tommy, you bastard, Tommy, it's me!' These words came from someone called Bruce who so far had said very little. Now he was animated. 'It's me cousin,' he explained. 'Me cousin Tommy Meredith. He'll see us right.'

The farmer swung his motor-bike round and roared down the field alongside us. The sheep reached the fence, turned and followed us. The Sikorsky and the Westland caught up too. Murray wheeled the Rover neatly about and left the choppers going in the wrong direction. Eric fired six shots out of the back window and both of them pulled sharply up into the air. Smoke was still pouring from the red Westland half a mile away.

Bruce leant towards the farmer out of the window and yelled above the noise of the engines. 'Those buggers up there are trying to do us in. We've got to get to Amber bloody quick. We can't use the road because they drop down and block it. Can you help us, mate?'

There were a large number of questions to ask but Tommy Meredith didn't ask any of them. For a full fifteen seconds he rode alongside us in silence. Then he said: 'Drive round the paddock for a minute while I nip over and open the gate into the next one. It's a straight run from there to the woolshed. I've got a twenty-ton sheep truck on hire and you should be able to drive right up the ramp and in the back of it. Nobody's going to try stopping on the road in front of that thing.' And he was away across the field without another word.

It may seem superfluous to say that the next few minutes were hectic but they were. There were two helicopters and several hundred sheep and the field, though large, was finite. The Land-Rover zigzagged across it in unexpected directions and the helicopters turned and turned again and never stopped firing, and the sheep stampeded madly from one side to another.

And then the gate was open and Murray put his foot down again and we made it through and it swung closed behind us. Tommy Meredith had disappeared, but in the distance we could see the shelter-belt and the woolshed and that meant safety: or something like it. The long yellow tussock parted as we passed like the Red Sea. We were half-way across when the Sikorsky dived at us.

One moment there were two of them, hanging in the air above us, and then there was only one, and the Sikorsky had tipped itself at us and was plummeting down out of the sky at an angle of 45 degrees.

It was the suddenness of the manoeuvre that did it, the shift in tactics. We were all frozen. I could almost see the muscles in

Murray's arms lock and his hands clamp themselves on the wheel. He wasn't going to be able to pull away. The chopper was going to hit us. Nothing could prevent a collision. Suddenly I understood why the Japanese believed in Kamikaze pilots.

The big blunt nose of the helicopter filled our field of vision the way the surface of the moon fills the screens as a lunar module comes in to land. For a few seconds I was looking straight through the scarred Perspex into the eyes of the pilot.

It was Karyanin. His face was a mask of pure fury, drained of blood, his lips pulled away from his teeth in a death's-head grin. It was like looking into an open grave. He wasn't going to pull out. He wasn't. And Murray couldn't. The Land-Rover and the chopper hurtled towards each other like the end of the world.

And then the chopper disappeared. Karyanin had chickened out. He had pulled the dive up short and we had driven under. We had won. Three seconds later the ground gave way under us and the Land-Rover dropped straight down into the stream.

They had stampeded us.

That should have been it, and it would have been if the same rigid muscles that had frozen Murray to the wheel as the Russians dived at us had not remained rigid, and if the people who had put the Land-Rover together had not done their job extraordinarily well. The Land-Rover bounced and bounced again in the middle of the stream, but it didn't stop and it didn't turn over and before any of us had picked ourselves up off the floor the damn thing was going again, accelerating downstream for the woolshed as if that was the way it was supposed to travel. We made a bow-wave like a battleship.

Three minutes later we could see the farmhouse, gleaming white amid green lawns, and across from the farmhouse, next to the dark shelter-belt, stood the woolshed. Next to the wool-shed stood the truck.

Then we were out of the stream and bouncing up the slope to the farmhouse, and I will always remember the sight of Tommy Meredith's wife walking out of the house to her washing line with a clothes basket full of washing.

She stopped stockstill, as the vision registered of the Land-Rover, battered beyond redemption, riddled with bullet holes and bristling with rifles, lurching out of the stream with two helicopters in hot pursuit. The basket seemed to fall from her hands in slow motion, the white linen spiralling elegantly out on to the lawn while her eyes and mouth opened in an expression of pure, unmitigated amazement.

There was a ramp, as Tommy Meredith had promised, at the back of the sheep truck, and we went straight up it and into the darkness. Our engine died, and as it did so the truck's big diesel sprang to life and its gears engaged and we began to move. We sprang out and jammed chocks under the wheels of the Land-Rover and hauled the ramp up till it formed the tailboard and we were shut in. By the time we had secured it we were on the road to Amber.

Chapter The Last: Amber

In case you've never seen one, a New Zealand sheep truck is a big lorry with what looks like a jungle gym on the back. This superstructure consists of two large cages made of weathered grey wood, an upper one and a lower one, into which sheep are jammed for their last journey to the factories, where they will be slaughtered and trimmed and frozen for the butchers' shops of Europe. The truck stank of sheep droppings.

The Land-Rover was on the bed of the truck, surrounded by the lower cage and covered by the upper one. We couldn't see the helicopters. But we could hear them. And as we watched, their bullets began to smash into the woodwork as if they had some grudge against the people inside.

'Business as usual,' said Eric, and picked up his .303. He poked the barrel through the slats and started firing. Everybody with rifles followed suit. When all the best spots in the lower storey had been taken, people began clambering into the upper one. The heavy throb of the diesel engine almost drowned the noise. Almost.

I turned to Bill and said: 'Bill, old mate, if they're not giving up now, when are they going to give up? They're surely not going to take on a whole town, are they? They must be out of their minds.'

'They are,' he said simply. 'They've got to be. You see, the problem is that they're in direct competition with one another. Neither side can give up now and let the other take the cake. As long as one of them keeps going, the other will too. And there's another thing. We've humiliated them. We've taken so much skin off their noses simply by getting this far, that it isn't funny. I think they're very angry indeed.'

'But they can't go shooting up a whole town. They've got to get out, they can't afford that, can they?'

'Right,' said Bill, 'absolutely right. But I've got an unpleasant suspicion they're mad enough to chance a little place like Amber. Its communications with the outside world will probably be poor, there probably won't even be a policeman, and if they can grab us and get out with minimum fuss, they will. In fact, when we reach that airstrip, it's going to be a close-run thing. Too close for me, I think: I'm done for, as far as any more ducking and diving is concerned. Too old for this sort of thing. Tell me, my friend, would you be prepared to take the variant? I'll make a note of the man to go to at the D S I R, and the chap at the Delhi conference. Would you do it? There's no need to spell out the risks. You know them as well as I do.'

There was a brief pause. 'I'd be honoured, Bill,' I said. 'I'd be honoured.' And I meant it. He took off the sodden belt and handed it to me. While I buckled it under the tatters of my shirt he scribbled with a pencil he'd found on the dashboard and handed me a scrap of paper. I shoved it into the belt beside the aluminium container.

I was a very rich man.

'Best of luck, mate,' said Sam. His face was a ghostly white, but the bleeding seemed to have stopped. We made our way to the front of the truck then and slid back the communication panel with the cabin. It looked as though an atomic bomb had gone off in there. The front windscreen had gone and the passenger seat was a gaping mass of foam rubber and shredded plastic. When Tommy Meredith glanced back at us his face was sheet-white, and a small trickle of blood ran down his forehead.

'I haven't enjoyed myself so much since nineteen forty-three,' he said. I never did work out whether it was a joke or not. 'Who are these bastards?'

He never got an answer. Suddenly the Sikorsky swept ahead of the truck and dropped like a stone on to the road a quarter of a mile ahead. The Westland joined it. There was no way round them, as there had been no way before.

Tommy Meredith put his foot down. 'Oh, you beauties,' he chuckled to himself. The truck thundered towards the helicopters and this time it didn't worry me at all. If I had been in the helicopters I would have been terrified.

They stayed on the ground for about ten seconds. Nobody got out. Then they went straight up in the air again. As they screamed past Tommy let out a wild whoop of delight. 'Like a couple of bloody magpies when I fire me shotgun,' he yelled. 'We'll be right, mate, another three or four minutes and we'll be there. The airstrip's just the other side of town.' Above us, in the woodwork, there was a fusillade of shots.

On either side of the road the fields looked tamer, greener, flatter and the first houses flashed past. A mile ahead, through the heat haze, Amber shimmered into reality. A minute passed, and we were there.

Amber wasn't a big place. It did have a main street, but it was the only street, and if there had been any competition at all it would have been hard put to defend the title. All the buildings in the main street were wooden, and all except one consisted of a single storey. Each of them had a tin roof, painted red, and a deep verandah with hitching rails. It looked as though it had been built out of the same mail order book they used to build Dodge City. There was a garage and a Farmers' Co-op store and a primary school and a War Memorial. There were three or four private houses and a couple of shops. At the far end of the main street stood the Imperial Hotel. That was the building with the two storeys, and I knew it was called the Imperial because its name was painted in great, white, faded letters on the red tin roof.

Beyond the pub the fields began again. In the second field floated the windsock.

We streaked right through Amber without a pause, until we reached the pub. There was nothing in the main street except three Holden station wagons. Two of them were parked outside the Farmers' Co-op. Two farmers' wives were loading them with provisions in cardboard boxes.

The third one had been parked beside the pub. Thirty yards

from the end of the street it drove unheedingly out into the middle of the road and stalled. Tommy Meredith jammed on the brakes.

It didn't look as though we would make it, but we did. The truck came to a halt inches away from the station wagon, and for a second all was silent. Nobody said anything, nobody did anything.

And then the Sikorsky dropped down on to the road in front of the Holden and the Westland dropped down on to the road behind the sheep truck. And this time there was no way out. Murray and Eric turned from their posts and looked at us. 'Sorry, mate,' said Murray. 'We didn't quite make it.'

'Hang on a minute,' I said. 'We bloody well will make it yet. Get the gear out of the Rover and get ready to lower the tailboard.'

'We won't get anywhere in that,' said Eric. 'The green chopper's parked about five feet away. It'd run right into it.'

'That's exactly what I intend,' I said. 'I'm going to try and make a dash for it, climbing out of the top of this thing. I want a diversion. When I give the word, would you open the ramp and run the Rover at them? What's the name of your mate at the airstrip, Murray?'

'Norm. Norm Bailey,' said Murray, 'but I'd better come with you. It'll save time. His plane's a blue and white job, registration T W 100.'

'Thanks, mate,' I said.

They started shouting through loud hailers then and hammering on the woodwork. I shook hands with Bill and Sam and clambered up into the rigging. Murray followed me. As we went, the hammering increased. I could hear Eric supervising the preparations.

Up on the top storey shafts of sunlight came through the cracks and bullet holes into the gloom. The floor was littered with cartridges. We began levering at the broken slats on the roof. Murray said: 'Better chance if we go separately, mate. I'll see you at the airstrip, right?' And I nodded.

We got the plank free and I swung myself up, outside and

into the sunlight. 'Best of luck,' said Murray. 'Same to you, mate,' I said, and then I was on top of the truck and on my own again, as it had been at the beginning.

The roof of the Imperial Hotel was about six feet away. It sloped steeply upwards. It was smooth, unbroken corrugated iron, and it offered no hand-holds. If I had had time to think about it, I wouldn't have done it.

I didn't have time to think about it. Down below, all hell broke loose.

There was a piercing creaking noise, and a thud as the tail-board hit the ground. Then there was a yell of 'Heave ho!' and a terrific rumbling, and the Land-Rover flew out of the sheep truck on its last joyride. It hit the Westland with an explosion like Hiroshima. I filled my lungs with air, contracted my body like a spring, and dived at the Imperial as I had never dared dive in my life. I hit it as though I had just jumped six hundred feet without a parachute.

I hadn't given myself time to work up my fear of heights when I was on top of the truck, but now I had made the jump I had all the time in the world. I landed flat on my face, six feet from the end of a near vertical slope, and began to slide straight down.

There are three sensations I remember apart from the fear. The heat of the corrugated iron after hours baking in the sun is the first one. The second is the feel of the paint as it smeared on to my face in a dry powder while I went down. The third is the noise that my fingernails made as they screeched uselessly on the tiny irregularities where one piece of corrugated iron is joined to another.

That slide took a long time, an unnaturally long time, but finally, as it had to, it ended. My feet touched the guttering and after the guttering there was nothing but a two-storey drop to the ground. As soon as my feet touched the guttering it began to give.

No fault of the guttering. It hadn't been designed to support thirteen-stone people and it couldn't. The nails that held its brackets to the walls began to pull out one by one, and as they did the guttering began to sag and swing out into the air.

I started walking along the guttering for the edge of the roof. With every step it pulled out of the wall. It was only a matter of time before the whole of it came away and I plunged down into the street. It was a matter of about twenty seconds.

At the end of the twenty seconds I was twelve inches away from the corner of the roof. I felt the nails pulling out beneath me and I used them one last time. I launched myself straight up the roof, arms out above my head, and as I did so the guttering tore out completely and clattered down into the street. By the time it reached the ground I had my hands around the corner-ridge and I was heaving myself upwards as if it had been a chin-up bar and I had been in a gym. If I had been in a gym I would never have been able to do it. But this was different.

When I reached the top there was a view I shall never forget. The main street of Amber looked like El Alamein. Great gouts of flame spewed out of the Westland, the Land-Rover, and the sheep truck. Even as I watched somebody fired at the Sikorsky and it went up too. Even on the rooftop I could feel the blast. That made three helicopters which wouldn't chase anyone any more. Especially me. All that I had to worry about now was the occupants.

I looked the other way, where the air was clearer, at the windsock and the airstrip. There were four light aircraft on the strip. Three of them looked as if they were asleep in the sun and would probably stay that way until rich farmers came along to fly them at the weekend. The third was taxiing out over the grass towards a fuel bowser. It was blue and white and its registration number was T W 100. I could have kissed it.

It was then I saw the trap door, half-way down the other side of the roof, and I went for it the way a wasp goes for a pot of jam.

I splintered all but one of my nails levering it up, but it wasn't for a long time afterwards that I noticed it. A blast of hot, dust-laden air rose out of the darkness. There was no chance of distinguishing what lay down there without accustoming my eyes to the dark, and there was about as much time to do that as there was to do a water-colour of the scene.

I just swung my legs over the edge and dropped down. The boar's head got me first, dead hair scraping down my leg, dead tusks tearing a small hole in my calf. I leapt away into a pair of antlers, and they turfed me neatly into a pile of magazines, thick with dust. They were called the *Auckland Weekly News*. The pile went over with me and the dust exploded into the air and spiralled up the beam of sunlight up to the trap. I lay there for a moment, half stunned, and an almost overwhelming desire swept over me to stay where I was, watching the dust dance and turning over the pink pages of the *Auckland Weekly News* while the glassy eyes of the boar and the stag stared at me thoughtfully and the sunlight slid in through the trap.

I fought off the desire. I got to my knees and then to my feet. I felt like a zombie. Then I began to go through the heaps of old boots, bottles, apple boxes and wire netting and carpets until I found the trap that opened into the main body of the building. I found it and opened it and looked down into the hall.

Even upside-down the hall was a small classic of tasteless parsimony, and I loved it. I didn't love it because of the bald, baleful carpet with two strips of non-matching flowered linoleum on either side or because of the white wrought-iron side table with its glass top and bowl of plastic flowers that looked as if they were made of Bakelite, or even because of the yellow varnished wallpaper with a D B Beer calendar of a girl and a cat. No, I loved it because it was empty. For about thirty seconds.

I dropped down into it and stayed where I had landed, while the thirty seconds elapsed.

The hall was no more than twenty-five feet long. It had three doors on one side and four doors on the other. All the doors were painted a cream colour, but that doesn't matter. What does matter is the fourth door. The fourth door didn't lead to a room. It led to the stairs, and there were voices on the stairs. Bede's voice. Murdoch's voice. And others like them. They were ascending the stairs.

A brief and vivid scene passed through my mind. I saw myself behind one of the cream doors and I heard each of the others in that corridor being smashed in turn, until they came to mine.

That was the end of that scene. I didn't care to take it any further. I got up and turned round. There was a window at the other end of the corridor. I walked silently up to it and raised the sash.

Outside, Karyanin was coming up the fire-escape. There were five men behind him. All of them carried guns. Smoke billowed up behind them from the street.

I stepped back into the varnished gloom of the corridor.

Panic was the big factor there. It rushed up my throat as though I was going to be sick, and I had to fight it down as though it were a physical thing. My hands were shaking uncontrollably. The panic only stopped when my mind started working again. It started when inspiration hit it, hard. My hand closed round the porcelain door handle behind me and I checked it would open. Then I started yelling at the top of my lungs.

It was what would have happened anyway, of course. I just speeded things up a little. Whichever side had got hold of the variant would have immediately been attacked by the other. The only thing that had kept them from each other's throats so far was the knowledge that the other side had not got it.

It was time to change that state of affairs.

'You bastards,' I yelled, kicking at the door-frame with everything I had and grunting in pain. 'All right, take it, take the thing, take it.' And then I screamed.

That was enough. Even before I stepped back into the room I saw the stair-door burst open and heard the clang of foot-steps on the fire-escape. Before I had the window up the first burst of firing reverberated down the corridor and before I was through the window the fire was returned.

They were massacring each other for the variant, and neither of them had it, and all I had to do was drop down out of a second-storey window.

It may occur to you that that is not a cinch, and normally that might be true. In fact it was true then, but I simply did not notice. I held on to the window frame, hung down my full length, and chanced the rest. I hit a bicycle frame and bounced off it on to the grass, and then I ran. I shouldn't have been able to but I could. It felt as though there was some utterly independent source of power in my legs. I leapt across the lawn, and there was a garden gate in front of me so I leapt that too. I went over the gate and into the field next to the airstrip and through the tall grass as if it was the waves by the seashore.

Through the haze I saw T W 100 move gently away from the fuel bowser and glide across the grass towards the fence which separated us.

I had a hundred yards to go when it turned its tail towards me and began to taxi away down the strip, and a brief and terrible fear ran down my spine that he did not know, that the plane would leave without me, that I would be stranded at the last. Then one of the doors opened and Murray stuck his head out and yelled, 'Come on, you bastard, R U N!' – and I did run; the fence came up at me and my legs grew longer with every stride, and I was up and over and pounding over the turf and the plane was bouncing along gently beside me. Murray reached out an arm and grabbed me. I jumped.

For a second I was half running and half being dragged by the plane, and then I was sprawled inside and Murray was shoving me into the third seat, and the grass flowed away faster and faster behind us, the eternal moment leapt at us and we were airborne. The plane tore itself from the earth's clutch and the ground fell away.

The township of Amber lay beneath us. It would never be the same.

The shooting must have finished because the main street was

full of people milling about the burning vehicles like ants, while black smoke poured into the air and began to drift westwards, back towards the mountains.

We were too high then, in theory, to be able to distinguish individuals among the tiny figures down there, but I distinguished. The two of them were propped up against each other in front of the burning helicopters and Bill had ripped the unutterable tatters of his shirt from his back, and he was waving them, high above his head, as though they were some brave, heraldic banner.

We levelled off then, in that peerless sky, and began to fly south.

More about Penguins and Pelicans